Perfectly
Flawed

DANI RENÉ

DEDICATION

To everyone who has ever felt like they don't fit it.
To all the girls, and guys, who were told they can't
do something, or they are not what society thinks
they should be. For every woman who would
rather wear a pair of Chucks, sweatpants, and
sport a messy bun.

You're all perfect in your own way.

This one is for you.

xx

BLURB

I was fourteen when I met him,
danced with him, and fell for him.
I was sixteen when Ryder left me with a forbidden
promise. Now I'm twenty, and he's back,
but he has a secret.

I walked out as the boy Piper had loved for far too long.
Now I'm back as a man who's broken,
angry, and flawed.
Yet, each time she looks at me, it's as if I'm perfect.

Can we have a second chance at love?
Or will our next dance be our last?

PROLOGUE
PIPER

The class before me watches my every move. Christopher, my mentor and boss, beams as he always does. The man who's become a teacher to me smiles with pride on his face. My body moves and sways, twists and turns. The beat of the song carries my feet through the steps without my mind having to think.

Lifting my foot, stomping it on the floor, spinning on one hand, I lock, pop, and glide into the positions. The kids shout and scream. They're excited for the upcoming show. So am I.

It's been years since I've not hurt. My heart

ached for four long years. I'm twenty and I've had my heart demolished by one person.

Most girls move on, find another boy, or man to fill the void, but I can never do that. Because each time I take the stage, every time the music pumps through me, he's there.

A ghost.

My heart remembers him. My very soul knows him better than I know myself. I wanted to stop dancing when he left. He walked away, leaving me with a goodbye and promises he never fulfilled. He never came home to visit when my brother, Preston, did, and he never kept the one promise he made before he left. The one boy I've loved all my life went to chase his dreams, and I didn't beg him to stay.

His life was his own. I had no hold over him. When he left to study in Los Angeles, he didn't just take the sun from my sky, he took my heart and soul.

I overheard my brother telling my parents

about life in the City of Angels. About how he, Jeremiah, and Ryder were on track to make it big in Hollywood in a well-known dance movie. But not long after his news, my brother was back home. When I asked what happened, he didn't want to talk about it, shrugging it off as nothing. I didn't ask outright, but when my parents brought it up, Preston said things didn't work out for them, and he wanted to come home to see his family. I knew it was bullshit because if there's one thing I know about my brother; he'd rather be anywhere but with family.

The song ends as I land in an open leg split on the linoleum floor. My chest heaves with ragged breaths. I'm smiling. It's a real one, more so than the other ones I've offered my family since Ryder left.

They didn't know about us. Not that there was anything to tell.

No, Ryder Kingsley was my secret.

The door to the studio flies open and just like magnets finding their mates, my eyes find his. My smile falls. His gaze hardens when he sees me, but there's a coldness to those pools I used to see affection in. And I'm no longer the girl who loves him, I'm a stranger.

"Piper, this is our new teacher, Ryder Kingsley. You'll be working on the show together," my dance teacher of three years announces happily and my heart that was thudding wildly in my chest drops to my feet like a lead weight.

This can't be happening.

But it is.

Ryder saunters forward with a slight limp, holding out his hand.

"Nice to meet you," he utters in that low husky tone I remember.

"Thanks."

And that's how the boy I fell in love with came back a broken man.

ONE
PIPER

It's in the moments you allow yourself to feel something, nothing can hold you back. That's what happens to me when I dance. Since I was little, being from an overly privileged family, I was sent off to ballet lessons. My mother said all little girls had to do it. As I got older, I filled out, got curves, and I hated those damn classical music snippets we had to dance to.

The day after I quit, I found myself following Preston to his secret meeting place. I didn't know what he and his friends did there, but something told me he was up to no good.

And I was right. He was drinking, smoking, and I would've told on him, if I thought my parents would care.

When Preston saw me skulking in the shadows, he called me out. That was the moment I found the two things I'd love for the rest of my life.

Hip hop dancing and Ryder Kingsley.

I was fourteen at the time and he was the forbidden older boy and brother's best friend, yet all I could do was think about him kissing me. I wasn't stupid to think a boy—scratch that, a man of seventeen, would want anything to do with a kid.

He was everything, with those deep hazel green eyes, full dusty rose-colored lips that had a small, silver ring pierced through the lower corner of his mouth. He had messy black hair and ink adorned his body, arms, chest, and back. With lean muscles, he was tall and overshadowed me each time he was near.

His smile.

That's what stole my attention. Bright, with slight dimples in either cheek. I later learned he was indeed the boy who'd grown up too soon. The boy who became the man who did what he wanted, after his father had forbidden him to do something he loved more than breathing. With a mother who could only love him to a certain extent, he focused on the one thing that made him gift me that smile—dancing.

He was alluring.

He was breathtaking.

He was perfect.

But I learned soon enough, he was flawed too.

Just like me.

It's how I always saw myself. The tomboy dressed in jeans and Chucks.

But each time my parents took me from his world and shoved me into theirs my heart shattered. My long blond hair was styled in a perfect chignon, my curves were draped in the finest silk, satin, and lace. It was my mother's dream as she played dress-up doll with her daughter for the world to see. She wanted me to attend all the formal dinners, dances, and every other party her friends told her about.

She would huff and complain when I mentioned a dance competition. She'd even scream and shout because I wouldn't go shopping at the most expensive boutiques. All the while I was growing up, I was torn in two.

Perfect in my world of skater shoes and sweatpants.

Flawed in the world of ballet lessons and fancy dresses.

That is, until I stumbled upon Ryder.

Somehow, we made sense. We didn't date, we didn't profess undying love to each other, but we did become friends. I couldn't explain why, or how, but he saw *me*. Not the glossed-up doll my parents wanted to parade around to all their friends. He saw the girl who wanted to dance and be seen as more than the polished ballerina that her so called friends saw her as.

We became comfortable, teacher and student. Friends. And that was all Ryder could offer me, or I could give him.

Nobody noticed when our friendship turned to something more. My brother was too focused on his girlfriend, smoking pot, and drinking until he passed out. Even though I was crushing hard on his best friend, my brother, didn't care. My parents were far too busy in their own lives to see what was right in front of them. Their innocent little girl was growing up.

When I turned fifteen, my folks finally accepted who I wanted to be. Not a ballerina, but a street dancer. However, with each comment my mother made, I knew she wasn't happy. I still went to fancy dinners, but I was also allowed to go to the warehouse to dance.

I spent every waking moment around Ryder. Even with my brother around, Ryder would find some way for us to sneak off somewhere, telling me to meet him out back where there weren't any prying eyes. When he looked at me, something changed, shifted inside me, and I was more confident in who I was.

And when he spoke to me in hushed whispers of how one day he was going to kiss me until I couldn't breathe, his words were engraved on my heart. It was then I knew he would always be there.

Ryder's hazel green eyes were something magical. It was as if he was trying to steal my breath with a single glance. And with those orbs that looked like leaves that just started turning on an autumn afternoon, I knew then I'd let him take anything he wanted.

It reminds me of the day I first saw him. The day my life changed forever. It was the moment Ryder Kingsley would burrow his way into my soul and forever be etched like a tattoo on my skin.

"What are you doing here, Pip?" Preston *smirks, strolling over to me.*

He's flanked by two boys who look the same age as him. My stomach twists with anxiety. I shouldn't have followed him, but I needed to see where he went every evening. The cigarette that hangs from his lips burns as the white smoke trickles up to the sky. My brother's blue eyes pin me to the spot and I'm paralyzed.

"I... Uhm..."

"Want to play with the big boys, little sis?" *he taunts. "Jeremiah, Ryder," he smirks at the two boys, "this is my kid sister."*

"Hey little girl, I'm Jer," *the taller boy without tattoos says. "Maybe I can teach you to bounce,"* *Jeremiah chuckles, rolling his hips in a sordid motion that can mean only one thing. I can't suppress the*

shudder that travels through me.

"Like fuck you will," Preston grunts, then pulls on the stick in his mouth. With two fingers, he pinches the object, holding it out toward me.

"No, it's gross," I respond, suddenly sounding much younger than I am.

All three of them laugh at me, but it's Ryder's cruel gaze that causes me pain. My brother has been mean to me all my life. That's not new. But these friends of his have never come by the house and I know why. If my folks saw their tattoos and piercings, they'd have a fit. And knowing my brother is smoking, I know for a fact Dad would take back the fancy car he got when he turned eighteen.

"Ryder, get her out of here. I have practice." Preston turns and saunters away from me, leaving his friend with the pretty eyes watching me like a hawk.

"What does he do here?" I ask the stranger who I now know is called Ryder. I haven't seen him before because I would've remembered someone so *handsome.*

He's tall. The vest he's wearing shows off his muscles and although they're not huge like some of those disgusting bodybuilders, he looks strong. Manly. The ink all over his arms and shoulders intrigues me and I catch myself staring at him.

"You shouldn't be here," he grunts, lifting a cigarette I didn't notice earlier to his lips.

My eyes are glued to his lips as they wrap around the thin white stick. His cheeks puff in as he takes a pull. The smoke doesn't come out for a long time, then he rounds his lips into an O and puffs gray circles into the air.

"I want to know what my brother is doing here," I tell him.

He doesn't respond. Instead, he walks by me and heads down to a black Chevy truck sitting in the parking lot of the skate park. He wrenches the passenger door open and turns to me. "Get in, Piper," he says smoothly.

"How do you know my name?"

"Everyone knows who you are," he tells me, shutting the door once I'm inside.

I watch him round the front of the truck and slip in beside me. The engine roars to life and soon, we're on our way. His hands tap the steering wheel to the song, but I can't take my eyes off him while he weaves us through the traffic. We're not far from the house. I could've easily walked home, but all I wanted to do was spend time around this man who's gained my interest.

"I guess with a brother like Pres everyone does know me." My voice drops sadly, and I glance out of the window as we pull into the drive.

"Hey," Ryder says then. "Chin up, little one, things aren't always what they seem."

The corner of his mouth lifts slightly, the movement causing his cheek to dip, and there before my eyes is a dimple. His eyes brighten at the movement. Raising his hand, he takes a lock of my golden hair and twirls it around his finger.

"Be careful of wolves, little one," he says,

causing a cold shiver to skitter over my skin. Gently, he tucks the strands behind my ear. The tender touch of his fingertips on my flesh leaves goose bumps in their wake.

It's the wolf who should be scared of the girl, *I think to myself.*

"I'm not scared of anything," I voice my response, but my tone is raspy, filled with nerves. My words earn me a grin and I'm bedazzled. He's otherworldly. The raven color hair on his head is disheveled. His tanned skin makes the greenish brown of his eyes even more striking. But when his lips part on a smile, nothing could've prepared me for it.

And in his truck, at the tender age of fourteen, I know for sure he'll be the first boy to break my heart.

I drag myself from the memory of the initial meeting I had with Ryder, the first time he ever touched me. When I felt the butterflies awaken in my stomach, it was something I'd never experienced before in my life. I didn't know it at the time, but it was the smallest moments we'd shared that would remain in my mind as I got older, and which, later in life, brought me to my first self-induced orgasm.

After that first time when I was seventeen, I was hooked. I chased the feeling constantly. I needed it, craved it. Each time I was in the shower, I'd trail my fingers down between my legs and I'd picture Ryder, his smile, his eyes, and the way he would always saunter with confidence through our house when he visited.

That night in his truck something inside me changed. When Pres came home, I asked him what he did at the park. When he told me he danced, I laughed, but he showed me his moves, and I was hooked. I begged and pleaded for him to teach me, to let me spend time around them, and one day he finally relented.

For months, I spent time at the skate park

with them dancing. And I loved it. After a year of seeing Ryder every day, being near him, it became clear there was a certain tension between us. It wasn't just me, because I recall he almost kissed me one day. We'd been doing a hand spin I couldn't get right. The moment I fell, he was there, lifting me up. Our bodies pressed tightly against each other, leaving me breathless.

I stupidly closed my eyes like they do in the movies, but the moment was gone when my brother sauntered up to us, chuckling loudly. He didn't notice the way Ryder and I were standing. He wouldn't have noticed if his best friend had me pinned down and began humping me. Ryder, however, was adamant that we were just friends. He made it clear when I asked him to teach me, telling me he would, and it would be as a friend. Nothing like getting your teenage heart trampled on before it had room to fly.

But something changed that night. I don't know what it was. The next day, Preston announced the three of them—he, Jeremiah, and Ryder—were moving out of their childhood homes and heading to finish their degrees in the city.

And that's when Ryder left me with a promise he didn't keep. It took me a while to get over, and even now, I don't think I truly am. I know I still love him, because I'll always love him.

Opening my eyes, I notice the sun has disappeared. There are thick gray clouds in the sky, hanging heavy with the promise of rain. Maybe even a thunderstorm. The house is quiet. There's never been a better time to be home than when my parents decide to go on their month-long vacations.

I watch as it gets darker with the impending storm. I love sitting out on the back porch. Closing my eyes, I take a few deep breaths. I'm lost in thoughts when a thud of the front door sounds, dragging me from my solace and back to reality.

"Pip!" My brother's voice comes from somewhere in our mansion. The place is bigger than a goddamn palace. "Where are you?"

"Out here," I call back to him. He's always called me Pip instead of my full name, which is Piper. At twenty, I'm no longer a child, but there are times I think of Ryder and I still get a flurry of butterflies in my stomach, which still makes me feel far too young to want him.

Preston's heavy combat boots thud behind me and I turn to find my older brother standing in the doorway.

"What's up, little pip?" He chuckles.

Did I mention my brother is an asshole?

"Nothing. Why are you home, Preston?" I question, rising to my feet. When I turn to face him fully, I realize he's not alone. Behind him are two other dark, brooding assholes. My brother's best friends. My breathing hitches in my throat when my eyes meet the familiar hazel green set that's staring back at me with pure venom.

Preston stalks outside, joining me on the patio along with Ryder and Jeremiah. Since I was fourteen I'd crushed on Ryder. His eyes that reminded me of leaves on the cusp of autumn, turning from green to brown. The way his smile tilted just enough to show off a dimple in his left cheek. The silver studs that adorned his lip and the one in his tongue always made me tingle and I wondered if he was pierced anywhere else.

"We're here to babysit you, little sister," Preston taunts me. Since he's three years older than me, he's always made it known that I was a mistake. He never had time for me when I was younger. He'd always leave me with Ryder and disappear with one of the many girls he had hanging off his arm.

"I'm old enough to take care of myself," I bite back, folding my arms in front of my chest. My gaze darts between the three, but it's those intense eyes of Ryder's that cause me to shudder when I notice they're pinned on my chest.

I stalk by him, slamming into his shoulder as I do, but his hand flies out to grip my arm. "Don't be bratty. I'm home. Deal with it," he tells me. All I can do is nod. Once he releases me, I head into the house and up the stairs to the safety of my bedroom. No doubt that tonight they'll throw a huge party and I'll be stuck in my room once more.

Shoving my shorts off, I step out of them and into a pair of gray sweatpants. If there's one thing my brother did right by me was to introduce me to dancing. Hip hop, to be exact. The love I found there, amongst the other dancers, was something I'd never had, not even from my parents.

I'm racing out of my door when I slam into something solid which knocks me on my ass. I yelp when my wrist twists catching my fall. Lifting my gaze, I'm met with the glare of Ryder Kingsley.

"Careful, little pip," he grunts out in a tone that's laced with frustration. "You shouldn't be running around without watching where you're going. You never know if the wolf will be there to catch you." The last few words bring a sinful smirk to his lips and I feel my nipples harden in response. He's had this effect on me for far too long. But since he returned he's been acting like I'm shit on his shoe. It's been years since he first walked into my life and stole my teenage heart.

"Perhaps I shouldn't allow animals in my house," I bite back my response.

Suddenly, his hand jerks out, grips me by the hoodie I'm wearing, and hefts me up onto my feet. Our bodies are close, too close for me to think straight, or even breathe.

"Maybe I like to be here. To see how angry you are with me," he tells me, his head tipping to the side as he hisses darkly into my face. "Remember what I told you. I fuck everything up. So, stop looking at me like I'm your world. What we had… it's in the past."

Anger simmers through me and I lift my chin in indignation. "That's the problem with you, Ryder, you're overly confident in what you achieve. You left once and I know you'll leave again. You were never my world." My words cause him to flinch, and I know I've hurt him. It's the slightest movement, but I see it. I see him. I've always seen him. "When you walked out and broke every promise you made me, you took every ounce of respect I had for you." My response causes him to chuckle.

His grip on my clothes doesn't relent. He leans in, his nose running along my cheek. The softness of the contact and the harshness of his hold cause my body to react like it usually does when he's around and goose bumps rise on every inch of my skin. "You should be scared of the big bad wolf, Butterfly. He likes to bite," he utters, then releases me, shoving me backward till my back hits the wall.

Emotion flits across his eyes, then he's gone, leaving me with a heart hammering wildly in my chest. *What just happened?*

TWO

RYDER

In the safety of the bathroom, I can't help recalling her reddened cheeks, the way her breathing hitched being close to me. But it was her words that hurt. They actually fucking hit me right in the center of my chest where my heart used to be.

As much as I wanted to lean in and kiss her, I know she's off-limits. Not because she's far too good for me, but because her brother would have my head if he knew about the things I want to do to her.

The problem is, I see how she looks at me. There's still that hint of want in her eyes. As if I can save her. I can't even save myself, let alone worry about another person.

But I can't deny that she still does something to me. She makes me want more. To be the person who can offer her the perfect life. It's been four years since I walked out and left her standing at the bus station.

When I turned and walked away, she broke. I knew she did because as the bus pulled away, I saw the tears streak her face. I wasn't good for her then, and I'm no good for her now.

But still, she offers me those fluttery eyelashes. She grabs my attention with the gentle sway of her hips. It's not noticeable to anyone else, but to me, it's everything. And she knows it's just enough to taunt me.

Being back here in this shithole of a town is like being drenched in a bucket of ice, but being in this house is even worse because she's just down the hall and I can so easily walk into her sweet smelling bedroom.

It's jarring watching her dance, seeing just how beautifully her body moves. When her dance instructor brought me into the classroom a week ago, the last person I expected was her, but I couldn't turn away. When I looked into those wide blue eyes, I prayed she'd moved on.

But she hasn't.

Neither have I.

It's still there, the electricity in the air. Emotion stealing the moments that pass between us. But there's no way in hell I'll touch her. My rap sheet is far too long. Added onto it what happened in the city, I know I can't bring that on her.

I made her promises I can't keep.

I gave her memories I now have to taint.

She can't love me anymore because I'm flawed.

Yet, each time she looks at me, it's as if I'm perfect.

I roll the silver stud of my tongue piercing

over my lower lip, biting down hard on the bar. Pulling my dick out, I take a piss with her still fresh in my mind and I find myself getting hard in my hand. Once I've finished, I shove myself back into my briefs, and zip up my jeans. Now I've got to go out there with a fucking semi because of Piper.

Washing my hands, I look in the mirror, my eyes are the color of a darkened lake. The green turning darker, but the hazel melding with it causing them to look bottomless.

Like glass.

Shattered, broken, fragmented.

Just like the man I've become.

Even after the night that changed my life, Preston still says it wasn't my fault. Like fuck it wasn't. I was there. I was behind the fucking wheel. Shaking my head, I inhale deeply, hoping to clear my memories of that night and every night after.

I lost everything. And now, I'm nothing

but an empty shell and I realize I need to own up to what I did. Every day I pay for a mistake that cost me not only my job, but the one thing I found solace in and that's dancing. Now, I teach kids how to do it. With time, I found comfort in knowing I walked away from Piper. She doesn't need this shit in her life. She doesn't need me.

I head back to the living room where Jeremiah and Preston are nursing two cold beers. The music booming from the speakers makes me want to dance. I remember the first time I saw guys moving, spinning, popping, I knew I needed to do it. But I no longer do it in front of them. They know why. And they've stopped goading me to do it.

"There's soda in the fridge," Preston tells me, gesturing to the kitchen that's just off from the living room and I nod.

"Thanks, man." I make my way into the immaculate space only to find Piper standing at the counter. Her body is stretched as she reaches for something in the top cabinet, but she's too short. Even with her on her tiptoes, she can't get a grip on the bowl.

Leaning on the doorjamb, I watch her for a moment. She huffs in frustration, spinning on her Converse heel. Her gaze lands on me, then those pretty blue eyes widen, and she yelps in surprise. "Jesus, what are you doing?" She gasps. Her breathy voice is linked directly to my cock.

"Getting a drink," I tell her, shoving off from the door, heading to the fridge. I pull open the steel door and grab a can of Coke. I snap back the silver tab and bring the can to my lips, taking a long, fizzy gulp. I can feel her gaze on me. She always watches from the sidelines.

Piper isn't one of those girls who likes to be in the spotlight.

"Can you help me?" she questions when I shut the fridge door and turn to leave. Her voice is gentle. Warmth settles over me for a moment before I remember who she is.

When I turn to look at her, those eyes, those goddamn blue eyes that seem to look right into my black fucked up soul pierce me. I don't respond. Instead, I close the distance between us. I lean in, cocooning her between me and the cabinet. I lift the bowl with a smirk on my face.

As I set it down, my eyes fall to her lips. Her tongue darts out, licking the plump lower one, and I have to stifle a groan. Her small white teeth appear, biting down on the flesh, and I wonder if they'll feel sharp biting my dick while she swallows it.

"Next time," I tell her, bringing my mouth to her ear, "say please." I allow my breath to fan over her skin, causing a slight shudder to race through her body. It takes all my restraint not to kiss her right there.

Stepping back, I turn and leave her in the kitchen. When I reach the living room, Preston's on a call to his girlfriend. The only reason I know that is because he looks like he's about to kill something. The blond bimbo who's been bouncing on his cock is only around for my best friend's money, so I'm not sure why he keeps her around.

"That Barbie on the phone?" I nudge my chin toward him as I talk to Jerry.

"Yeah, apparently she's crying or some shit. Seriously, he needs to sort this shit out. I'm sick of her messing with our time. Also, the whole dating a bad boy thing she's doing because of her dad is getting real old."

"Yeah, that's true." I nod, not really interested in what's going on with Preston and his girlfriend.

Jeremiah gulps down the rest of his beer, while I sip my Coke. It's been two years since I ever let alcohol pass my lips. I vowed to never go back there. As soon as I touch a beer, I know I'll never forgive myself for my actions.

"Are you coming down to the park with us? It's been two years, man." Jeremiah's always been a good guy, a friend who understands and listens. Whereas Preston has been the asshole of us all, but something tells me there's a lot more underneath his dickish exterior.

"Nah, I'll catch up with you tomorrow. I think I'll just chill here for a while and then head home."

He nods, but his eyes tell me a different story. He's not happy that I'm giving up everything, but he can't understand what it feels like to be glared at.

When people see you're different, they judge, they snicker and gossip, and that's the last thing I want or need.

Preston flops onto the sofa across from us, sighing dramatically. "Jesus, I promised myself I'd never break up with someone over the phone, but it had to be done." His blue eyes glance over at us. He has a satisfied smirk on his lips.

"What are you going to do now?" I ask, curious as to why he'd break off a relationship with the blonde who followed us from Los Angeles all the way to the Pacific Northwest with its cold and dreary weather just to see him.

"I'm going out tonight to get laid," he informs me with a grin.

Pushing off the sofa, I make my way to the patio door.

"You okay, man?"

"Yeah, I'm just tired."

"You can take my room, just don't jerk off on my bed." He chuckles.

That earns him a laugh from me. "Why not? Thought you loved me?" I taunt, knowing that most girls have begged and pleaded with him, saying the exact same thing. But Preston is the type of guy that will hit it and run. Before their eyes open the next morning, he's out the door and heading home. Even though there have been times where he'd had a *girlfriend* none of them stuck around for too long.

We've known each other so long that nothing is secret anymore. Since we were fifteen we'd been friends. Like brothers. Now, at twenty-three, I don't recognize him anymore. Fuck, I don't even recognize myself.

"Oh, baby, you know it," my best friend responds in the girliest tone. "Hey, come here, Pip," he hollers at his sister, and my body goes rigid. I hear her light footfalls as she enters the room. "Make us something to eat. Sandwiches will do." His order is abrupt, and I want to punch him for talking to her like that.

"Why can't you do it yourself? You've been living on your own for four years, surely you can make a sandwich?"

"Don't be snarky, Pip. Or did you want me to say please?"

"I'll do it. I need to get another drink," I

say, turning to the room. I step by her, catching a scent of her perfume that smells like apples. Sweet and delicate.

In the kitchen, I pull open the fridge and grab the butter, cheese, and tomatoes. As the door swings shut, she's standing on the other side.

"I said I'd do it," I bite out, but she doesn't bat an eyelash.

She makes to take the tomatoes, which are slipping from my grip. "I'll help," she offers, setting them on the counter. I watch her get the bread from the container and we work in relative silence making six sandwiches. Carefully, she slices them into halves, and I grab one. Biting into it, I notice her gaze land on my mouth, then she lifts those pretty blues to meet my hazel eyes.

"Thank you," I tell her, and she scrunches her nose at me talking with food in my mouth.

"That's gross." She giggles, and the sound

causes me to forget how much I should push her away, and I smile. I give her the one thing I know she's wanted since I walked in here today.

I shrug in response, eating the rest of the sandwich before grabbing another. She shakes her head and leaves me to go to the fridge. Once she's packed everything away, she gets a Coke from the fridge and sets it down beside me on the counter.

"I don't know what happened, but..." Her words taper off and her face falls for a moment with sadness in her expression. "I hope you'll trust me enough to tell me one day." With that, she grabs the plates and leaves me dumbfounded in the kitchen.

I remember the one day I told her a secret. I trusted her with something I'd never even told her brother, or Jeremiah.

"If you keep your leg straight, you'll be able to

lean back and flip," I explain, holding her hips with my fingers digging into soft, smooth skin.

She's dressed in a pair of low-slung sweatpants and a sports bra, which in turn shows off her toned stomach. Since she's been dancing, I've spent most of my free time teaching her.

"You got it?" I ask, stepping back.

"Yeah." Her voice is raspy and I wonder if she's as affected by me as I am by her. I know nothing can happen between us, but that doesn't stop my mind wandering to places it shouldn't.

I head back to the chair and sit back, lifting the remote, I turn the song back on loud. The song starts and Soulja Boy starts singing "Kiss Me Thru The Phone" —it's the song she's been begging for me to teach her moves to, so I do it. It's been almost two years since she first got into my truck and I find myself doing anything she asks. Even though she's almost sixteen, far too young for me to be having the dirty thoughts I have about her, I can't help be intoxicated by her laugh, her excitement, and her *shining blue eyes.*

I watch her move across the mat in the abandoned warehouse we've been practicing in for years. She dips, rolls, spins. Her body was made for this, to move, to dance, to flow, and each movement is like a hypnotic drug to me.

When she lands on her hands and her legs open in an upside down split, I'm hardening and I have to drag my eyes away. Fuck. She's only fifteen and all I want to do is kiss her, touch her, see what she looks like coming on my fingers.

"How was that?" She laughs, righting herself as she bounces over to me.

I nod, my mind still in the gutter as she settles herself before me on the floor, cross-legged. At times she looks so young, so beautiful and breakable, and at other times, she is strong and resilient.

"You were made for this, Butterfly," I tell her, catching myself on the nickname.

She notices immediately, her cheeks darkening as she smiles up at me. I see it. Those glistening jewels she pins me with. She likes me, and as wrong as it is, I bask in that. I want her eyes on me all the time.

"What's wrong?" She creases her brows in worry and I shake my head. Somehow, she sees through me, noticing the slightest change in my demeanor. "Tell me, Ryder?" She shifts onto her knees and I stifle the groan that rumbles in my chest. She looks beautiful kneeling between my legs.

For a year I've been good, I've been responsible as we've worked closely together. Soft touches, gentle words, and now, we're alone and everything shifts as she peeks up at me from under her long golden lashes. Her chest heaves as her breaths turn ragged.

"This… We should go."

"No, I know something's wrong. Is it your parents again?" Her question jolts me from wanting to kiss her to fleeing as far away from my life as I can get. She knows about the pressure I'm under from my parents. They want me to be the perfect

son and go to Harvard to study law and follow in my father's footsteps. Since I chose a different path, they've been at me constantly, forcing me to spend time at my dad's offices to see what I'm missing out on. All I've seen are stuffy suits who are fucking their secretaries for some excitement in their lives.

"I'm leaving, Piper," I tell her. "My father told me that if I don't do as he asks, I'll be disowned, so I applied to study with a dance studio in Los Angeles. I can't be around them anymore."

"But… what am I going to do?"

"I'll always be here for you, but this is my life. The problem is, I did something stupid when I was younger. Well, a few stupid things. It was long before your brother and I became friends," I confess. I remember the night so distinctly.

Her hands are on my knees, holding on to me tightly. My heart riots against my chest, slamming painfully, causing my breathing to come out huskier than I intend. She's so close, too damn close.

"You know you can trust me," she tells me, and

I nod.

"When I was fourteen..." My words are tentative, but I know I can tell her anything. Somehow this girl has found her way into my heart. She's become everything to me, which is wrong on so many levels, but I can't stop it. "I almost overdosed because of depression. I..."

"Oh God," she cries, leaning in. She wraps her arms around my neck, our bodies flush against each other, and suddenly she's on my lap. Holding me as if I'd break without her. And I realize at that moment, I will. Without a doubt, I'll fucking shatter if she ever leaves my life.

That was also when I knew I had to leave. If I needed her this much, she might feel the same and I can't do that to her. Her small tits are squashed against me, her legs over mine, straddling me. I don't think she even realizes what she's doing without doing anything at all.

"I'm so sorry, Ryder," she mumbles into my neck, the heat of her breath tingling over my

skin, and my cock hardens unbidden. I can't stop it. I can't make it go away and any second, she'll notice it. That's when she shifts on my lap and a soft gasp falls from her lips. "Ryder?" She pulls away, meeting my hungry gaze.

"You need to get off me, Butterfly," I murmur, using the nickname I've given her. She moves across a dance floor like she's flying, like a beautiful, delicate butterfly.

"Are you...?" she whispers, dropping her gaze between us. The sweatpants I'm wearing don't hide the erection that's tenting them and she gasps once more.

"Piper." Her name is a warning on my lips. "We can't do this. Friends, remember?" I close my eyes, attempting to think of anything other than the beautiful girl on my lap. I need her to move, or I'm going to do something stupid, but for the life of me, I can't lift her off or move her. I can't do anything because I'm frozen.

"Ryder," she moans my name and I can't stop

myself from gripping her hips as she rolls them on my lap. Her heat against my thickened cock.

My head drops forward, leaning on her shoulder as I try to rein in my need. My restraint is a thin string that's pulled taut, about to snap. "Jesus," I hiss as she grinds herself on me. Soft whimpers fall from her plump lips.

"Promise me you'll never do that again," she whispers in my ear as she continues her ministrations. The song changes and R. Kelly starts singing "Cookie" and as the bass vibrates through us, Piper mewls as her body shudders all over me and I have to bite down on my lip to keep from coming in my sweats.

I watch in awe as she trembles in my arms, on my lap. She's beautiful, like a blossoming flower in spring. Everything about her is light, happiness, innocence. Her lashes dance along her cheeks as her eyes roll back. When she finally opens them again, they're glistening with excitement.

"Do what again?"

"Hurt yourself," she mumbles, with a pout on her full lips. She's still perched on my lap. My cock is still rock hard, but she doesn't seem fazed.

"Please, Butterfly, you need to get off me." I hear the pain in my voice, not because I don't want her, but because I want her too much.

"Did I... Was it... I mean..."

"You can't, we can't do this," I tell her, noticing the unshed tears pooling in her eyes. "Hey." I cup her cheeks, holding her face so she can look at me. "I'll be in big trouble if I so much as touch you, so please, baby girl, don't make this harder than it already is." My words cause her to giggle, dissipating the tension that hung heavy between us seconds ago.

"It is pretty hard," she says shyly as she moves off my lap, giving me a reprieve of her gentle apple scent. She turns the iPod off. "You know, I've thought about that a lot." Her confession stills me for a moment.

"What?"

"Your hands on me. Making me feel good." Something about the way she says it and what we've just done makes me smile. I've wanted to touch her for far too long. *"Would you promise me one thing, Ryder?"* she asks, turning to face me again.

"Anything for you, Butterfly," I tell her, and I mean it.

"One day, when I'm old enough. I want you to take it." I know what she's talking about, but I play dumb. Mainly to hear her say it, to give me the words I crave.

"Take what, baby girl?" I question with a smirk and she chucks her towel at my face. I catch it easily.

Then her face falls serious. *"I want you to be my first."* Her words turn me molten and I'm tempted to say fuck it and do it right here for her, but I know she deserves more. And if I'm in prison for fucking her, I can't be here for her when she needs me the most, and right now, I need to be a responsible adult, even though all my restraint is pulled tight. So, I nod in response to her. *"Promise me, Ry? You*

54

need to say the words."

"I promise."

THREE
PIPER

Stepping into the classroom, I find Christopher corralling the kids into lines facing the large mirror. This is my internship, and soon, I'll be a fully-fledged dance teacher. I hope one day I'll be able to have my own dance school, where I can teach hip hop to as many kids as possible. My mother would've preferred me to teach ballet, but I'm no longer that girl. I never was, to be fair.

"Ah, Piper." Christopher smiles at me when I enter the class. "Kids, sit down on your spot. Remember, back straight, head up," he demands with a wide grin. The tall, dark-haired man has been working here for most of his life. With dark brown eyes and a friendly smile, he offered me a bear hug the first day I started. It's been almost two years and I've never been happier working and learning from him.

"Good morning, Christopher." I offer a smile.

He leans in to give me a hug, and I return it easily. The man is affectionate, so much so that at first I thought he was flirting, but when he met Preston on one of my brother's visits, I realized his eyes were for the same sex, and not for me.

"Are we working on the show today?"

He nods. "Yes, Mr. Kingsley will be here soon. He's going to observe today. He would like to see the skill level of the children and he'll be working out the routine," Christopher gushes and I can understand why. Ryder is the best. At least, from what I remember.

"Great."

"Isn't he just so handsome?" my mentor says with a sigh. As if he could sense we're talking about him, Ryder saunters into the room.

His eyes find mine as soon as he's near and my cheeks heat. He's always had this effect on me. Something I could never stop, never hide. But he told me once, we're just friends, that I was too young for him.

"Mr. Kingsley." Christopher smiles. "So good to see you. I was just explaining to Piper that you're going to be here to observe today. I trust you'll be comfortable?"

"Yes, I'm looking forward to it." Ryder shakes Christopher's hand, and I'm sure the older man is about to melt into a puddle on the floor.

"Great, I'll leave you to it." As soon as I'm alone with Ryder, the air is heavy with tension.

"So, you're back?" I question, setting up

the stereo. The soft whispers of the kids are the only other sounds in the room beside my breathing. It's so clear that he still makes me nervous.

"I'm back for a while. I'll be heading to LA once I'm done here to open a studio of my own," he tells me with a confident tip of his chin.

"Wow." I turn away, knowing the tears that prick my eyes will tumble if I keep looking at him. Pride for what he's accomplished makes me emotional and I want to hold him. I want to tell him how much I still love him, but I can't.

"Yeah, so, what were your plans with the song for the showcase?"

Shrugging, I turn to the class and clap my hands. "Okay, my lovelies, let's get up and start stretching," I tell them to a chorus of squeals. They love the class and it's their happiness that makes me smile every day I walk into this room. "I was thinking of something fun, perhaps a pop song of sorts."

"I'll watch your warm-up and then we'll talk about the music," Ryder informs me, settling on the seat beside the stereo. "How about you show them our warm-up?" He suggests, causing my breath to hitch.

"You remember it?"

He stares at me for a moment. The coldness in his gaze tells me he doesn't recall it for the same reasons I do. No, we're just friends. But the way Ryder is looking at me now, I don't think we're even friends anymore. What hurts is that I don't know why.

"Piper, this isn't time to run down memory lane," he bites out.

Stalking toward him, with rage burning through me, I lean in, so my face is level with his. "If you're going to be in my classroom, I suggest you leave your assholeness outside. Are we understood?"

His gaze burns bright at my retort. Desire

flickers there briefly, then, back to the cold hardness that is Ryder's new expression. "Let's start the class," he utters, crossing his hands over his chest, pinning me with a severe glare.

Spinning on the heel of my sneaker, I turn to the class that consists of five boys and seven girls. They're all so passionate about dancing and love it when we experiment. Attempting to ignore Ryder glaring at me from the corner of the room, I start the class, giving them the new steps we're learning this week.

I press the button on the remote control and the song pumps through the speakers. I want to look at Ryder, to see his expression, but the anger at his aloofness holds me hostage. I no longer want to play this game with him.

He was the one who walked out, I was the one who waited, and he acts like I've hurt him. But I'm the one who's hurting. I have been for four long years and he doesn't care. When he left to go to LA, I spent my time focused on dancing. I chose to teach it rather than be on stage because this is where I can guide those who feel like I did when I was younger. Alone, frustrated at having to strive for perfection in a world that just wasn't.

"Okay, that's perfect," I tell them with a smile, watching them count as they move in sync to the song. It took a while for them to work as one with these steps, but practice has made them master the moves in no time. "Now, I want you all to meet our new instructor. He'll be helping us with the showcase that's coming up," I tell them excitedly.

"Yay! Is he a famous dancer?" Brianna, one of my girls, questions.

"He is super famous, and you know what?" I tell her. "He was the one who taught me how to dance. He made me love everything about it."

The class goes wild with squeals and each of them leaping around like I've just told them they've won a year's supply of candy.

"You shouldn't lie to them," Ryder whispers in my ear, causing me to turn my attention on him. His eyes are dark green today. The hazel color is gone and there's only frustration evident in those familiar orbs.

"I didn't. Not about dancing, and not about love. You did make me fall, you just weren't there to catch me." Without waiting for his response, I step farther away from him and turn toward the kids, clapping my hands. "Okay, everyone say hello to Ryder."

Even though he's livid at me, he smiles down at them, answering questions and telling them about his time in Los Angeles, teaching at one of the schools there. He tells them things he's never even bothered mentioning to me.

And my heart breaks just a little more for the boy who returned a broken man.

FOUR

RYDER

I should have never come back. It took all my restraint to not kiss her today. But my anger at the way she looks at me, is enough to make Piper understand I'm no longer the boy who walked away. I can feel her pain when I bite out my responses at her.

She's always been an empath, feeling my pain and agony, but this time, we swapped roles and I hated every moment. I don't want to hurt her, I don't want her to break even more than she did the day I left.

Shoving the door to my apartment open, I step inside to find Jeremiah and Preston already settled on my sofa, both gripping PlayStation controls like their lives depend on it. The speakers screech and I recognize the sound of cars racing.

"Shit," Preston grunts. "Fuck, Jeremiah, stop being an asshole." He sways toward our best friend and I can't help chuckling. I've known both of them nearly all my life, and I couldn't have asked for better friends. Even though we'd fucked up on occasions in the past, we still stood by each other.

"Pres, why don't you get your ass out of my way." Jer chuckles, and a loud crash thrums through the speakers. It's been a long while since that sound would send me spiraling.

"Are you two fucking up my high score?" I question, sitting my ass on the armchair, far from the couch where both guys are practically shoving each other off the cushions.

"Jeremiah's being a pussy ass bitch as usual." One thing about Piper's brother is that he loves cussing. If he could've gotten a degree in it, he would've.

"Yeah, sure, Pres," Jer announces. "And I'm the one losing, am I?"

"Fuck off," Preston bites out, tapping the buttons as if hitting them harder would make a difference to the game.

Shaking my head, I rise and head into the kitchen. "Did you guys fill my fucking fridge with beer?" Silence meets my question and I can't help the frustration flowing through me.

"There's soda in the bottom drawer," Jeremiah finally responds, and I find a neat stack of cans in a corner. "Can you grab me a drink please, bro?"

"Yeah." I instinctively take two cans, along with my soda, to the living room to find my friends sitting back, the game on pause and both sets of eyes on me. "What?"

"How was school?" Preston asks, cracking open the can. I know what he means, *how is*

Piper, but he doesn't voice the question.

"It was fine. Kids are damn good for being ten-year-olds." I watch them watch me and I wait for it. Both Preston and Jeremiah know about Piper's crush on me, and they also both know I've held a forbidden flame for her for years. Only, Preston's never given me his blessing to come back and be with his sister. Not that I deserve it, because everything I touch turns to fucking ash. And Piper is far too precious for me to burn with my sins.

"And your little blonde?" Jeremiah takes the chance to ask me, their eyes searing me with unasked questions.

"She's okay. Doing a great job with the class."

"Don't bullshit me, Ryder," Preston smirks, sipping his beer. "I know you have the hots for my sister. Everyone knows it. So don't sit there and tell me it was just like any other day."

"It was. I told you, Pres, I'm not back here

to start a fucking relationship."

"You didn't tell her, did you?" He shakes his head, the guilt eating away at me because he's right. I should've told her the moment I returned, but I'm too much of a fuck-up to confess what I did.

"Why would I tell her?"

He glares at me, anger simmering just below those blue-green eyes that are a mixture of mine and Pipers, a strange mix, but they're unique to Preston.

"What?" I take a swig of my soda, ignoring his penetrating stare.

"Just wondering why you're so fucking scared to tell her. Piper is not going to judge you for what happened. If anything, she should blame me." He's right, but that doesn't mean shit to me right now.

"Play the fucking game, asshole." I tip my can toward the television.

"Preston is right, man," Jeremiah offers.

"She's a sweet girl, she loves you, and there's nothing that is going to make her change her mind or her heart for that matter."

"Fuck off, Jer. Don't talk about my sister being in love." Preston acting like a big brother is strange, which only makes Jeremiah and me chuckle.

"I'm dead serious, Ry," he tells me, his dark brown eyes locked on my green ones.

"Doesn't matter," I tell them both, "she's out of my league."

"Too fucking right, she is." Preston nods, and I can't help chucking a cushion at his head in frustration.

"Fuck you, Pres."

"You wish," he retorts, taking a long gulp of his drink. Turning his attention on me, his expression turns serious, before he continues. "You need to tell her."

"Yeah, I know." My response is sobering in so many ways because I know I need to come clean. She has to know what I've done, what I've been through, and I need to tell her why I never came back for her eighteenth birthday. I broke a promise and that guilt will sit heavily in my gut forever.

FIVE
PIPER

There isn't a moment in time that doesn't remind me of Ryder. When I turned sweet sixteen, as he put it, he brought me a gift. A present that, to this day, I keep with me at all times. When we spent time together, dancing, practicing moves, he used to call me *Butterfly* and sometimes, I felt like I was.

An awkward little girl, a teenager who didn't belong in the crowd her parents had forced her into. I was a tomboy, but even through that, he saw me. Glancing in the mirror, I drag my gloss over both lips, making them shimmer.

My eighteenth birthday has long since passed and so has his promise, and now that I'm almost twenty-one, I know what we did that day will just be a long lost memory.

The day I asked Ryder to take my virginity flits through my mind. I was nearly sixteen and it was just before he left. He promised me that on the night of my eighteenth birthday, he'd be there and he would do it. And as much as some of my friends had already given theirs away, I knew mine was already his. I knew since the first day I saw him.

Only, he didn't return for my birthday. He didn't keep that promise. And now, he's back, he's angry, and the boy I loved is a hardened man who seems to have forgotten what he felt for me.

The baggy blue sweatpants I'm wearing hang low on my hips, and the matching sports bra holds my boobs perfectly. I'm slight built for a twenty-year-old, but I'm proud of my body. My white skater shoes adorn my feet and I'm ready to see him.

Soon, I'll be heading to Los Angeles to dance. I've been counting down the days. Three long weeks to go. But before I can walk away from this place, I need to fix what's broken between us. Even if he doesn't want me anymore, I need to say my piece.

When I overheard Preston and Jeremiah saying they're going clubbing, Ryder said he was going to hang out here and then head out. I know where he'll go. It's the one place he loved spending time. The warehouse where we practiced night and day.

My long blond hair is tied in a messy bun atop my head and the fine strands that hang down, framing my face, twirl into soft waves. Ryder told me once I looked like *Goldilocks*. And I retorted jokingly that him, my brother, and Jer were the three bears, looking out for me. As much of an asshole as my brother is,

I know if something did ever happen to me, he'll be there.

Grabbing my phone, I slip it into the pocket of my baggy sweatpants and head out the door. The house is quiet, barren from life. Just like this town. Even though Dad wanted a corporate career, it was my mother who won out and since he owns half the restaurants in the country, they can live off the income and never see their children. I think they planned it that way. No responsibilities. No worries.

I hop on my bike and make my way down to the large gates of our estate. The security who sits in the office all day smiles and I offer a nod. The roads are quiet at this time of the evening and I can't help smiling at how peaceful it is. As much as I'd love to see Los Angeles, something about this place always holds me back.

A small town in the middle of the Pacific Northwest where the sun hardly shines and the gloomy gray clouds hang heavy for most of the year. There are so many things in life that seem dreary since he left—school, my family, or better yet, my parents, this house. The only things that haven't changed for me are dancing and Ryder—the two things I've loved almost all my life.

Most girls my age are out partying, driving into Portland to get drunk and do drugs. I know because I've heard the stories. The one friend I made in school, Sienna, was the only person who understood my need to be a homebody. But she's taken her scholarship and headed to New York. I haven't seen her in over a year, and we've only ever chatted a couple of times via email. Since she's been there, she's changed somewhat, become more of a party animal than I ever could be.

I am the good girl. The one who spends her nights in her bedroom studying. Focusing on things that don't include going out and getting gloriously drunk. I've managed to keep myself healthy and free of anything like that.

The cool breeze sends a shiver through me and I realize I should've gotten a ride from Preston. But I didn't want him to know where I'm going.

When I reach the warehouse, I notice his truck parked right up against the door. Smiling, I feel my face heat up despite the cool breeze. Locking my bike against the railing of the steps that take me up to the main section of the large building. Pulling my hoodie up over my head, I hold it in my hand before entering the large space.

Before I push the door open, I hear the music booming through the space. It's loud, the bass vibrating everything in the vicinity, and I wonder why he has it that loud.

The building is derelict. Cold. Barren.

Since the day he left, I've thought about this place every minute of every day. After what happened between Ryder and me in this place, I've never been able to come back without him here. It might sound stupid, but being here without him didn't feel right.

There's never been a more poignant time for him to come back and for me to find myself here with him. This was the place I had come on Ryder's lap. He didn't touch me, he didn't move. It was me who'd broken our code of trust as friends and allowed my body and feelings to take over.

But it was also the place he promised to be mine, to be my first. And part of me is scared of him leaving again. Watching him walk away is something that has gripped me since I saw him at my house earlier.

When I step inside the warehouse, I hear the music vibrating through the columns of steel. It echoes through the vast room—bass, drums, and a rapper. Dirty, sexy, and so damn intoxicating. My body wants to move. It begs me, pleads to follow the beat, but I don't. I close my eyes and revel in it for a short moment before moving closer.

I knew he'd be here. No matter how many years we spent apart, I still know him better than anyone. Better than Preston or Jeremiah. When he stepped onto the porch earlier, I knew I couldn't avoid him. My heart thuds to the beat of the bass. It remembers the movements, the rolls, pops, and every other step I made with his hands guiding me.

The song changes and I recognize it immediately. "Cookie" by R. Kelly echoes through the speakers. His deep rumble sounds incredible coming from the two subwoofers that are plugged in behind the man moving in the slivers of light coming through the shattered windows.

The song is one we've danced to before. The beat races through me. I feel every second of the bass. I recall the day clearly, straddling Ryder like he was a goddamn chair. His hands on my hips gripped me so hard, I had bruises for days. It was one of the most intense, sensual moments of my young life. The lyrics are dirty, naughty and I can't help blushing.

When I reach the open area where we used to practice, my eyes are glued to his form spinning, dropping, and locking. His hips move sensually as he gets lost in the song. Those beautiful hazel green eyes are closed, entirely one with the music.

Pop and roll. One. Two.

Flow. Three. Four.

Bounce. Five. Six.

Spin. Seven. Eight.

His body is glistening with sweat and I can't help licking my lips. I've wanted to kiss him for years, and I only got one chance. He gave me two quick, stolen kisses when I was younger—just a taste of the sweetness I craved before he walked out and left with my brother. Black sweatpants hug his hips. They hang low enough for me to see his V-line muscles. He isn't wearing a shirt and his tanned, toned torso ignites a yearning so deep inside me, I can't catch my breath.

The tattoos that adorn his arms look like they're alive with the beat. A large dreamcatcher sits on his ribs, and I wonder if it hurt. His body is still utter perfection. Just like it was when I first saw him without a shirt on.

He's wearing a baseball cap. It's low, hiding his shimmering eyes. I notice the black and silver skater shoes that adorn his feet. I know they cost a small fortune. Element x Etnies Jameson Vulc. Every kid out there who dances wants a pair of those.

I should tell him I'm here, but I don't. Instead, I watch in awe as he moves. There's always been something magical about the way his body flowed with the beat. Perhaps that's why I was so enamored with him.

He's lost in the music, in the rhythm. A

small smile plays on my lips. It lifts the corner of my mouth until I'm grinning like an idiot. My heart slams against my chest at the sight of him when he comes to a stop. His body tight with tension, his legs spread high in the air, and his arms taut as he holds himself upside down. He lifts his head infinitesimally like he can feel me, and that's when he sees me.

He pins me with a glare so fierce, so damning that I'm sure it will send me straight to hell. The music surrounds us like an entity, a force living and breathing, magnetizing us. And at that moment, I decide I need to move. My body easily picking up the steps that are ingrained in my very being as I slide toward him. I spin, drop to my knees, then roll on the floor, keeping him in view each time I do a three-sixty. He, in turn, responds by dropping onto his chest, rolling toward me.

We move in sync as I jump to my feet, spinning around him. His hands find my hips.

They hold on to me, lifting me in the air as he spins with my arms and legs straight as if I'm flying. He drops me, sliding my body down his sweaty, naked torso. His scent is intoxicating, reminding me of cinnamon and spice.

The music reaches a crescendo. I'm sweating. So is he. It's sensual. Sexual. Dangerous.

We move together like lovers.

Familiar, yet estranged.

We dance. We gasp. We combust.

Silence.

We're both breathing hard.

My chest is flat against his. His hands still hold on to my hips. I don't move. I can't because he's close, too close. Our gazes lock. My heart slams in my ears. I'm almost deafened by the vibration, but his breath—that soft, calming sound—is the only thing I can hear.

"What the fuck are you doing here, Piper?" His voice is raspy as it rolls my name on his tongue like he's caressing me. And I wish he would. All I've ever wanted was to feel his lips on mine. A teenage dream of having your crush kiss you.

"I…" My voice is croaky when I respond. Clearing my throat, I try again. "I needed to see you," I tell him. His eyes, those green and hazel orbs, glisten with a mix of emotions I can't place because they move as fast as he does in battle. When he's dancing against another person, he's like a damn soldier.

"You shouldn't be here. If he knew you were here…" He doesn't need to finish the sentence because I know I'll be in a world of hurt if my brother finds out I'm currently wrapped in Ryder's arms. But I'm no longer the little girl with a crush on my older brother's best friend.

I'm meant to be an adult now, old enough to know right from wrong. He's twenty-three, and he *should* know better. We've been through all this before.

"Are you telling me to go?" I ask. My head tips to the side in question. Electricity sizzles between us, crackling from the top of my head to the tips of my toes. He stares at me for a moment longer before his lips quirk into a grin.

"I'm telling you it's wrong for you to be here, Butterfly." He smiles, the nickname he loved calling me all these years still present. I'm acutely aware that his body is still pressed against mine. My heart is still thundering in my chest.

"You walked away, Ryder. You made a promise that day." The words are a whisper, but he hears me. He can't not. When he leans in, my breathing hitches in my throat. His lips feather over my ear, grazing his teeth over the fleshy lobe, as he suckles it into his mouth.

"You still taste as sweet, Beautiful." He says the word *beautiful* like it's my name. A slight movement and his mouth finds my neck. The spot just behind my ear tingles when he presses a gentle kiss to it. "It's time for you to go. You shouldn't have come here," he tells me once more, reminding me that he was the one who walked away, leaving me to live with a broken heart. To be stuck in this limbo of not knowing if he'd come back. Not because of his promise, but because in the two years we'd spent together, he became more than just my brother's best friend. He became my first love.

He walked away when all I did was beg him to stay, but I was a naïve teenager. Over the years, having him gone has given me strength, but seeing him today, the agony that's so clear in his eyes makes me curious as to what happened in the city.

"You didn't miss me, Ryder?" I'm taking privileges. When he looks at me now, there's no longer that boy I knew when I was fourteen. No. In his place is a man with a broken soul. But then again, I'm no longer the little girl who had her first orgasm on his lap. I'm grown up, different, changed more than he could ever imagine.

When I look at him now, I see how much he's changed. He's harder, colder, more rigid. He doesn't answer for so long, I wonder if he heard me, or if he'll give me a response. My heart aches. It physically hurts in my chest to see how much the happiness from his time with me has dissipated, and in its place is someone I no longer recognize.

"Piper, missing you is what... it's what I've been doing for four years. No. It's what I've been doing since I first saw you," he informs me. Stepping back, he finally releases me from his vise-like grip. He turns away, looking at the view of the city below us instead of meeting my gaze.

"What do you mean?" I want to go to him, but there are too many things we need to talk about before things go back to normal, if they ever do. He's been away for four years.

Perhaps in that time, he's found someone new. Another girl he loves. The thought knocks the breath from my lungs and tears sting my eyes. As much as I think I've grown up, deep down I know around Ryder, I'll always be a teenage girl.

The realization stills me, and I drop my head. I never should have come here. There's no point in begging someone to love you because it's something that should come naturally. Surely, if he felt the same, he wouldn't be pushing me away.

"I better go, it's getting dark," I tell him, turning away from his rigid form. The tension in the space is enough to choke me. Even though we're in a warehouse triple the size of our home, it feels as if I'm in a matchbox.

"No!" He growls, stalling my escape with one word. I cast a quick glance over my shoulder, allowing hope to flurry in my chest like the wings of a butterfly.

"I can't have you back in my life," he tells me. His back is still toward me and his shoulders are tense, his hands fisted at his sides.

"Did you ever love me?" I ask outright.

Honesty was our promise to each other. Lies only got in the way, so Ryder and I made a pact when we started dancing together. When he became my teacher, trainer, and when he made me fall in love with him. We vowed to always tell each other the truth. And when he left for the opportunity to study with one of the best dance studios in the city, I let him go because when you love someone, you don't hold them back. You send them on their way with the courage to do it. Not that he needed it. Ryder Kingsley has been a rock through all the years he's struggled with depression. I'm the only one who knows how bad things actually got for him.

We found our only refuge in dancing. He

taught me how to use my body to move to the beat and I taught him how to let go of the pain in his mind. Ryder drops his head for a moment. A sigh is the only sound from him.

"Yes." One word, brutally honest. The love of my life. And the only man who broke me. When he left, I couldn't bring myself to be with anyone else. He was mine and I wasn't moving on. Sienna said I was stupid to hold out for a man who'd clearly moved on, but deep down, I knew Ryder wasn't like my brother. Somehow, I knew he wouldn't just go out and find a girl to sleep with. "You should go, Piper," he murmurs. My name on his lips sounds foreign. I know he's serious when he uses it.

"I don't want to. You made a promise to me, Ryder. Are you going to keep it?"

He spins on his heel, facing me once more. Hazel eyes pin me with heat, hunger, and desire. His body glistens in the low light. The setting sun bathes us in an orange glow that makes it seem as if he's on fire.

Ryder Kingsley.

My temptation in black sweatpants and skater shoes. Looking at him now, you'd never guess he was once a boy of fourteen wanting to end his life.

"If you stay, I'll fuck you," he tells me, but he doesn't move closer. "And I don't know if I can be gentle right now. Because all I want to do is steal your sweet virginity. That same innocence you asked me to take all those years ago, Butterfly," he says. "You deserve better than me breaking you roughly in a warehouse." His mouth tilts just so, causing his normally hidden dimples to appear in each cheek. The man is deadly, not only on the dance floor, but with that stomach fluttering smirk.

"You've always had a dirty mouth," I retort with a smile of my own.

There's nothing around us for miles. The forest sits to the left, and to the right is the main road that brought me here, which only takes us back to town. We're back in the one place that gave us everything. I never understood how something so beautiful can come from something so ugly.

"You love my dirty mouth," Ryder confirms. "Come, I'll walk you out." He reaches for the tank top that's lying on the speaker, and I make my move. Stalking toward him, I stop only inches from where he's now straightened to full height. "Butterfly," he says, a warning in his tone. That same warning he gave me all those year ago.

"I missed you," I tell him honestly, my eyes peeking up into his. There's nothing more I want than his lips on mine. Just once. Even if it is only one kiss for the rest of my life, I'm sure I could survive.

His gaze falls to my chest and he steals my breath with the heat in his hazel green eyes. I know what he's looking at the moment he reaches for it and lifts it from my body.

"You kept it." His words are whispered in awe.

The small gold butterfly pendant I've worn every day for the past four years has never left my sight. I've held it on lonely nights, and I've had it hanging from my neck each day he was gone. And now that he's here again, I wore it for him.

"It's the best birthday present I ever got. Sweet sixteen, remember?"

He nods at my words, then turns away as if he's angry, but the tension radiating from him tells me there's more to his reaction than I think.

"Ryder..."

He looks at me then, the tee still in his hand when I reach for it and drop it back where it was. Finding the courage, I pull the tank top I'm wearing up. Once it's on the floor, my black sports bra is the only thing I'm wearing, besides the sweatpants that have a matching pair of panties to my bra underneath.

"Jesus, Piper." Ryder runs his fingers through his short-cropped hair. "I can't do this now." He's at war with himself. The bulge in his sweats tell me one story, while his mouth voices another. There's tension in his muscles, in his arms.

I take one more step and lift my hand, settling it on his bare chest, trailing my fingertips over the smooth tanned skin, along the lines of the ink that adorns his flesh. The wolf that's inked on his neck peeks at me, howling at something, and I wonder if it's the pain Ryder's been through. The significance of that one piece of art is breathtaking.

"I can't stop if you keep touching me," he warns. His eyes burn through me. All those nights in my bed thinking about him, about how he would feel on top of me, his body between my thighs. I fantasized about him more times than I can count.

"And if I don't want you to stop?" I question. My head tips to the side, watching him for an inkling of refusal. But he doesn't offer it. He doesn't move.

"We can't do this here, I can't… We can't… Fuck," he hisses. Spinning on his heel, he stalks away from me. My hand falls to my side, and my heart aches in my chest.

"We don't have to do anything, Ryder. I just want to know what's going on with you. You're blowing hot and cold."

"Listen to me, Piper." He turns, his eyes casting a warning glare over his shoulder. "I'm not the boy who left. I've changed."

"And I'm not the girl you left, Ryder. We all grow and change, but—"

"There are no buts, Butterfly!" He growls his response, causing me to step back in shock. He's never been so adamant or so harsh with me. But this right here is something the new

Ryder has become. A cold, hard man I no longer recognize, but sadly, I still love.

SIX
RYDER

"Why are you pushing me away?" Her question is pained, raw and emotional, and it rips at my heart more than I care to show her. I'm not right for her. I'm a broken man who has no right to claim her.

I can't face her. My body vibrates with anger, need, and the desire to kiss her until she can't breathe. To steal every breath of her innocence and taste every flavor of her heart and soul. Shaking my head, I stalk toward the shattered window and look out over the forest that sits behind the warehouse.

All my life, I wanted something good,

something that was mine. Not given to me by my parents and not offered to me by friends. But mostly, I needed to grasp onto something that held me steady and that one thing is right here, and I can't take it. My choices in life have made sure I can't have a girl like Piper.

"You need to leave, Piper," I tell her once more, but she's stubborn. She won't walk away from this until I hurt her. It's the last thing I want to do. Seeing the tears in her eyes is not what I want, but I don't have a choice. She needs someone who can give her a happy life, not someone like me.

"Listen to me, Ryder. Whatever's happened—"

"Jesus, Piper!" I bite out, spinning on my heel. "Just do something I ask you to do!" My voice booms through the vast space. It vibrates through my chest. My throat is raw with emotion, with the agony of telling her to leave me. Her gentle gaze turns so fucking sad, I feel it rip my heart from my chest.

"You know something, Ryder?" she retorts hotly, stalking toward me with anger flashing in her pretty eyes. Her pink painted fingernail pushes against my chest as she prods me with her index finger, and I let her. I want her to hurt me. "I never pinned you for an asshole, but you're just like my brother."

Her words hurt because I've always wanted to be better than Preston in the sense of how he treats her. But right now, she's exactly right. I *am* an asshole.

"Why did you come back, Ryder?" She taunts further. "To fuck with me? To mess with my head and break my heart? Well, I'll tell you something." Her eyes fill with tears. They're ready to fall. One blink and they're streaming down her face, causing tracks of sadness on her pink cheeks. "You've already broken my heart, time and again, and me? I'm the fucking idiot who let you. No more."

The venom in her words jars me. I've never heard her curse. Never. And now she's spitting the words as if it means nothing. Her body visibly vibrates and I realize she's freezing. Her skin is dotted with goosebumps.

"I didn't mean—"

"Fuck you, Ryder!" She interrupts me, spinning on her heel.

I watch her grab her top, shrug it on angrily and stalk out of my life, leaving me with nothing more than an aching chest. Sighing, I rush toward her, hoping to catch her before she can get on her bicycle. I know it's the way she would've gotten here. She's always loved that old thing.

As soon as I reach the door, I step outside to find her struggling to unlock the chain. She's pulled on her hoodie, hiding her curves from my gaze. I take the stairs tentatively, not wanting to make her even angrier than she already is.

"Can we start over?" I ask gently. I need to get her home safely, then I'll leave and not look back. I'll head back to LA and she can be free of me.

"Why?" Her hands on her hips make her look guarded, as she should be. "Tell me, Ryder. What is the point of me giving you a chance to make it up to me? Only for you to rip me to shreds again?" Her question hangs between us and I want to rip it from the sky and trample it to the ground.

"Just let me take you home at least? It's cold. You're going to get sick," I tell her, hoping to make her see I'm right. She's silent, her lips pouting in that sweet, sexy way that makes me want to claim them. To devour her mouth, tasting her.

"Fine." She finally gives in and I nod.

"Let me grab my keys and we can go," I tell her, but she doesn't respond. Instead, she pulls her phone from her pocket and taps out a message to someone. Jealousy flares to life in my mind and I wonder if there's someone else in her life. No. There can't be. She wanted me. She came here for me, so there can't be another guy.

Turning, I head inside. My phone and keys are beside the stereo. Once everything is turned off, I head back outside and unlock her bike from the railing. As soon as I make sure it's safely in the backseat of my SUV, I open the passenger door for her. Before she settles in the seat, she pins me with an angry glare but doesn't say anything.

In the driver's seat, I steal a glance her way, wondering what's going on in her pretty little head. Her cheeks are no longer wet and I'm thankful she's stopped crying. Putting the car in drive, I pull out onto the dark road. It's going to be a long fifteen minutes to get back to her house. Reaching for the radio, I turn on the system and we're met with the melodic voice of Jay Sean singing "Cry."

Every lyric he sings feels as if he's taking a stab at Piper and me. A soft sniffle comes from my left, and I look over to see her shimmering cheeks in the dim light of the almost non-existent sliver of moon above us. I stop the car, pulling up onto the side, and kill the engine.

"Piper—"

"Just take me home, Ryder," she says softly, her voice thick with emotion. "I can't do this." Her words are pained, and I know I've done this. I've hurt her and I have to live with it.

"I'm sorry," I tell her then.

She turns her head, meeting my guilty gaze with her teary one. "Why did you come back?"

"I don't know," I lie. I can safely say it wasn't the pressure from Jeremiah and Preston. But I do know I wanted to feel normal again, and the only way I could do that is by seeing her again. And now that I have, I realize it was a mistake. Being around her only confirms I'm not normal. I never will be again and I should stop trying.

"You've never been a good liar," she says, looking right through my façade and seeing the darkness, secrets, and guilt that sit like a lead weight in my chest.

"No, I haven't. But your choice in guys is something you need to work on," I joke, hoping to lighten the mood. Because as much as I want her to be happy with someone else, I still miss her smile. I want her to remember me in happier times.

"Ryder, I'm probably too young, maybe I don't have enough life experience, but…" her words trail off, her fingers twisting the material of her top. When she meets my gaze once more, she smiles. "I will always want you," she confesses.

The words cause my chest to tighten painfully. I want her as much as I did years ago, but I'm not the same person I was then.

"I'm sorry," she mumbles quietly.

"Never be sorry for being honest," I urge her. "Look at me." When she turns her head to me, I cup her cheeks in my hands, reveling in the silken skin below my fingertips. "I fucked up, Piper. I'm not the same person I was four years ago." It's the most I can give her because the truth is something I'll never be able to offer.

"Then why don't you trust me enough to tell me what happened?" Her big eyes implore me and I can see the desperation in her expression. She needs me as much as I need her, but I don't know how to be that boy she fell for.

"It's not that I don't trust you." I sigh, sitting back against the leather seat. I look out at the dark road and wonder where the fuck I'm heading. My life has changed drastically because of what I did, and my dreams are no longer feasible.

"Then what?" she questions.

I can't respond, so I don't. We sit in silence,

looking through the window at the blackness that envelops us in its cold uncertainty.

I reach forward, twisting the key to start the engine. A soft purr. Nothing more can be said. I can't offer her what she needs. If she knew what I've done, Piper would never look at me the same again. I drive her home with a heavy heart. The agony grips me painfully. It feel as if time has stopped at this moment.

She exits the car without saying anything. I watch her walk up to the door. She's left her bicycle in the back of the car and I wonder if she's done it so she can see me again. Perhaps to ask me to come back and bring it to her. Once she's inside the house, I get out and open the backdoor.

Tugging her bike from the car, I set it at the entrance where she'll see it. It's a goodbye. It's a farewell to the person I wanted to be with her. Sighing, I hop into my car and head back to the house I grew up in.

Being home has many disadvantages. With my parents' home, it's like being in prison. All this time, I've run and run. Now there's nowhere else to go. I'm stuck here because I can't face reality. I can't come clean.

"Ryder," my father's strict tone comes from behind me. His face is rigid, his posture as well. The lawyer who makes millions a day, who doesn't care if his family is falling apart as long as he can play golf with his buddies. The man who cheats on my mother every day he walks into his office. The one person I hate more than myself. Henry Kingsley.

"Dad," I respond without a smile. We're not on good terms. We've never been. When he doesn't say anything else, I head up the stairs. As soon as I reach the landing, that's when he decides to throw a snide comment my way.

"I trust you'll leave that little girl alone. She's far too young for you." He turns and leaves me staring at the empty space he's just vacated. Asshole. My friendship with Piper came easily, but he is the only one who noticed how close we got over the years.

Maybe that's why he didn't care when I said I was leaving. Perhaps he wanted me gone so I wouldn't do something stupid with her. Only, I did. I allowed her to become attached, but most of all, I fell in love with her.

My bedroom is on the opposite side of the house to everyone else and I'm thankful for that when I shut the door and exhale. I should've gone to the apartment I'd rented when I arrived, but I need to be closer to her. A few doors down is the house that had been off-limits to me growing up, where I know Piper will be sound asleep in her room while I sit on my balcony thinking about her while I smoke my cigarettes.

Seeing her today in those low-hung sweatpants and tank top did nothing to quell the urge I have to fuck her. She begged me to take her virginity. She'd wanted someone she could trust, but deep down, I wonder if that was a good idea.

I could've done it. Right there in the warehouse, I could have lifted her against me, driven my dick into her, and then walked away. Or I could just walk away now and let her lose it to someone who'll hurt her worse than I ever can. Both options make me an asshole.

Flopping onto the bed, I place both hands under my head and study the ceiling. The patterns I've looked at since I was ten swirl above me. I want them to take my mind off her, but nothing will. Nothing ever does.

My phone buzzes and I lift it to find her name in big black letters staring back at me. I don't think twice about unlocking the screen and tapping the message.

Hi, this is Piper. You can call me Butterfly. So far only one person does.

I can't help the grin on my face from her

message. It's a mirror version of the first text message I ever sent her.

Hi, this is Ryder, but you can call me Asshole. Most girls do.

I hit respond and tap out my response.

Tell me, Butterfly, what are you doing right now?

The three dots bounce as she types out her reply and I find myself invested in this. I'm not sure why she's doing it, but it seems to ease the tension between us.

Lying on my bed, wondering if someone's thinking about me.

What if he is thinking about you?

Then maybe he should stop acting like an asshole and call me.

I chuckle at her sassy response. Tapping her name, I put the phone to my ear and listen. It rings three times before she finally answers.

"Hi, asshole," she says, but the smile in her voice is evident.

"Butterfly," I murmur. "You're so bad for me." My words are an honest, raw confession.

She's silent, then I hear her sigh. "And you're perfect for me." Her softly spoken words only serve to make me want her more. To need her here in my arms where she was always meant to be.

"I'm flawed, baby girl. I'm broken."

"Then we can be perfectly flawed together," she says in a hopeful tone and I wonder if she could be right. "I've never wanted anyone else, Ryder. It's been you, it will always be just you." There's a small glimmer of hope in my chest. With each word she utters, it ignites into a flame flourishing into a wildfire.

"I can't give you what you want," I tell her, hoping to keep the pain from my voice. I shut my eyes, wondering what she's doing. If she's sitting in her window seat or if she's in bed. It's late, and she should be sleeping, but the selfish part of me doesn't want to let her go.

"And what if you can? Unless I don't mean anything to you." Her voice sounds small and the gruff rumble from my chest must tell her I'm annoyed at what she's just said. She has no right to think that about herself.

"You mean everything to me, Piper. But, as they say, if you love something, let it go…"

"And if it comes back you'll know. You came back, Ryder." I can hear the urgency in her voice. Her plea. She's begging and I can't deny I want to be with her. To give her everything she's asking for.

"Good night, Butterfly. We'll talk soon."

Before she can respond, I hang up. Pushing off the bed, I head downstairs to the kitchen that still looks as if my mother just walked out, leaving it spotless. She was the one person who enjoyed being a family. My father never wanted me. At least, it felt like he didn't all my life.

"Ryder." My father's voice comes from the

doorway. "You're to stay away from the Beaufort house. I know you and Preston are friends, but the girl is off-limits. Do you understand me?" My father used to be a handsome man, with those green eyes, dark hair, and his sculpted features. My mother used to gush about how many women wanted him.

But now he looks aged. Not because he's older, but because it seems like life itself has taken its toll on him.

"Dad, I'm twenty-three. There's nothing wrong with me spending time with Piper. She's an adult now, and so am I." I've always kept my relationship with Piper platonic. Even when I noticed her crushing on me, I fought my feelings and made it clear to her that we were just friends. I recall the day I told her. I could see the tears she blinked back, shrugging it off like it didn't affect her, but I knew it did.

"I'm looking out for you. I know you may not think so, Ryder," he says, closing the distance between us. He places a hand on my shoulder, squeezing it, and I know that's my father's sign of affection. "I just don't want you to get hurt."

"Why would *I* get hurt?" My question stills him for a long while. The look in his eyes tells me there's something he's holding back. A secret.

"I've made many mistakes in my life, Ryder. And, as much as I know it's part of life to learn from those mistakes, I don't want you to fall into the same trap I did."

My brows shoot together in confusion. "What do you mean?"

"Just please be careful," he says, and my heart crashes into my ribcage. Something's wrong and he doesn't want to tell me what it is.

"I'm always careful, Dad, but you're worrying me." This time, I pull him into a hug, and it's the first time in almost ten years that my father holds me, slapping my back in a *man hug*.

"I may not always be here, and I haven't been the best father, but I do love you, son." He stares at me for a long while and I know he means it. I can see it in his eyes. We've been estranged since my mother left, but right now, this feels like he's finally accepting me.

"I'm going to be staying at the rented apartment downtown while I'm back here. I just wanted to get a few things from my room tonight."

"I understand." He nods. "Just know the house is always here for you. The door will always be open if you need to come home."

"Thanks, Dad."

He leaves me in the kitchen to mull over what just happened. He's clearly hiding something from me, that much I know, but I can't help smiling to myself at the show of affection from the man who's always been cold and standoffish toward me.

Grabbing a soda, I head back to my bedroom to pack a few things I want. Tomorrow I'll be on my own, and even though my childhood home is still here, it's time for me to move on.

SEVEN
PIPER

I haven't seen him in two days.

After the call, I overheard Preston talking on the phone about Ryder heading back to the city. I don't know if he said it because he knew I was eavesdropping, or if his best friend really is gone. I did go to the warehouse, but it was empty.

My heart hurts thinking about him just walking out of my life again. Even though we're not a couple, I still have feelings for him. Wishing them away didn't work, and my attempt to move on is frivolous at best. Each time a guy asks me on a date, I'd compare him unfairly to Ryder. I recall the day he walked out. When he left and I knew for certain he wouldn't come back.

The sun is hiding behind thick gray clouds. It's the final day and I don't know how to say goodbye. Ryder leaves along with Preston and Jeremiah, and something tells me he won't be back. Yes, promises were made, but I have a feeling he'll be happier without me. He'll forget the little girl with the crush on him.

I don't blame him. He's older, more mature than I am. At least, that's how I see it. When he goes out to clubs in Los Angeles, he'll have hundreds of girls swooning over him. I shake the thought out of my head, hoping with all I have that he'll tell me he's decided to stay. Call it wishful thinking or whatever.

Pulling on the hoodie, I stuff my feet into my sneakers and head out the door. I'm meeting him at the warehouse and we'll be walking down to the bus station together. Since Preston left earlier, and Mr.

Kingsley took Ryder's car keys, he's having to take the bus.

I know my brother would've come back and picked him up, but there's one thing about Ryder — he's far too proud to ask for help. It's not far to ride, and I take my bike to the place that's become a second home to me over the past couple years. I needed Ryder when I didn't think I needed anyone, and now he's leaving.

Moments later, I stand my bike beside the door and step into the large open space. Finding Ryder dancing in the dim light of the warehouse, I watch him for a moment, and I can't help smiling.

I close the distance. My eyes are glued to his body moving like it's fluid with the song. It's a slow one, and watching him do a spin on one foot is strange. He's doing pirouette, but he's dressed like a bad boy with ink adorning every inch of bare skin.

I close my eyes and listen to the lyrics as if he's trying to tell me something with the song. "Feels Like Home" by Chantal Kreviazuk is beautiful and heartfelt. My heart aches in my chest at the thought of him leaving today and I need to blink back the tears.

As soon as the song comes to a stop, so does he. Ryder's eyes find mine, and we're tethered. It's as if he can always sense where I am, and it doesn't matter how crowded the room is, or where I am. He will find me.

"You're early," he says, stepping up to me, pulling me into a hug. The warmth he always radiates cocoons me in such a way that I find myself tearing up again.

"I'm late. We better go." My words are mumbled into his T-shirt, but I know he's heard me because he steps back.

Cupping my face with his hands, he holds me steady, leaning down so we're eye to eye. "No crying," he demands. "I don't like seeing you sad, Piper. I have to do this."

"I know," I tell him, swiping at my wet cheeks. Lifting my chin in defiance, I offer a sad smile. "I'm allowed to miss you."

He nods, as if allowing this to be my excuse when he knows it's so much more. Then we're moving through the warehouse, collecting his things. We take a walk down to the main road where the station is, just outside town.

"You know; I'll be back before you know it. You'll probably be dating some asshole," he tells me chuckling, earning him a swat on the shoulder. "I'm serious, Butterfly," he croons my nickname, making my body tremble.

Just then, a bus comes to a standstill at the terminal and we're in the rush of a crowd of people heading out to a better life while I'm stuck here with parents who don't love me.

"Promise me, Ryder," I implore. "Tell me you'll come back for me."

He smiles, his dimples appearing, and I can't stop my mind from taking mental pictures of him. I need to remember him like this, happy, smiling, like a man about to embark on the adventure of his life.

"I will be back for you, Piper, I'll always come home for you." The emotions swimming in his hazel eyes steal my breath, stop my heart, and turn me rigid. I blink, the tears flow, and I know I'll never stop crying, not until he comes back.

"I love you." I've never said those words to anyone before. Ever. But it feels like the right time to finally tell him. He knows. I know he does.

"And I love you too, baby girl," he tells me, leaning in to plant a kiss on my lips. And then he's gone, leaving me with tears streaming down my face. It dawns on me that he didn't hesitate to tell me he loves me.

Picking up my phone, I press my thumb to the reader to unlock it and open my messages. The last one from him is from two days ago. Just before he called me. Then, silence. I push off the bed and make my way into the kitchen. The coffee is already brewing, the space smells like the cafe down the road.

"Pip," my brother calls from behind me. When I turn around, I find him leaning against the doorjamb, staring at me. "What are you doing today?" he questions, stepping into the immaculate space. My folks ensure that the house is always shining and spotless. Well... what I mean is they have staff who do it for them.

"I have classes today, Preston. You know that," I tell him, crossing my arms in front of my chest, annoyed that he doesn't remember anything I talk to him about.

"Don't act bratty, Pip. I need your help with something," he says, grabbing a mug, which he sets beside the coffee machine.

My gaze follows him as he fills it with dark liquid, then takes a long gulp before looking at me again. "What is it, Preston?" I sigh, thinking he's about to ask me to call up one of his girlfriends to give her the boot. He's done it before, and even though I thought he was an asshole, I did it for him because he's my brother.

"I'm worried about Ryder," he says, causing my heart to kick against my chest. When I meet those familiar blue eyes that are a mix of mine with a hint of green like Ryder's, I see real emotion flickering in them. His eyes hold something I've never seen on my big brother's face before—concern.

"You're *worried* about him?" I laugh, turning away to grab a mug and fill it with coffee. "That's a first. Who are you and what have you done with my asshole brother?" I question.

"Look, I know I've been a pain in the ass for most of your life, but… he's my best friend." This time when I look at Preston, I see it. He's hiding a secret. His eyes dart back and forth between me and the mug.

"Tell me what you're hiding," I demand, but my voice is barely audible. He's silent for a long while and I wonder if he heard me, but then he sighs. Leaning back against the kitchen sink, he watches me for a long while. "Please, Preston. If something—"

"It's not my story to tell, Pip," he finally responds, interrupting my questioning. "This is up to Ryder to tell you. If he wants to. I know you have a thing for him."

"What?" I gasp, swallowing the shock I know is clear on my face.

He shrugs, then smirks. "Come on, sis... Do you think I'm blind? Every time he walks into the room your cheeks burn a bright red. Your eyes follow him around like a lost puppy."

"Don't be ridic—"

"You're saying I'm lying?" This time my brother looks like he's far too satisfied with his assessment.

I open my mouth to respond, but I can't. I'd be lying to my brother and as much of an asshole as he is, I can't bring lies into our already volatile relationship.

"I thought so." He nods. "I don't care about your crush, or his, for that matter, as long as he doesn't hurt you. Or else I will have to kill him." It's the first time my brother has ever shown any concern for me. For my well-being.

"What's changed between us, Pres?"

"Nothing. I've been through shit while in the city. I've fucked up a lot and because of that, my best friend is angry with me. He may not show it, but it's my fault that his life is now as fucked up as mine is." The agony that drips from his words is enough to have me stalking toward him. Placing a hand on his shoulder, I give it a squeeze, which makes him look at me.

"What happened?" I ask again, knowing he won't offer up the truth, or the story, because I'm certain Ryder is the one who needs to tell me.

"I told you, Pip. It's not my story to tell. Ryder is the one you need to hear it from. He loves you, you know?" This time, Preston stares at me, his expression serious. There's no glimmer of a lie or a joke.

Ryder does love me?

Once again, my heart thuds, beating out a melody against my ribs. "He doesn't. I'm just his best friend's little sister."

"I've seen him attempt to date other women when we were in the city, but nobody makes him smile the way you used to."

"Used to," I tell him. "Those are the operative words that describe me and Ryder."

"You'd be so surprised to know he still holds a flame for you. Trust me, just this once, Pip." My brother smiles, his eyes crinkling at the corners. There's nothing that can prepare me for what my brother does next. His arms wrap around me, pulling me into a fierce hold. "Give him a chance to explain. Don't shut him out just yet," he tells me. "And don't give up on him. He may have made a mistake, but so did I. He, however, has paid far too long for his."

"What's happened to you, Preston? You're scaring me with this cryptic nonsense." This time, my words earn me a chuckle. My brother, all six-foot of him, is every girl's dream. With his blond hair, blue green eyes, and those dimples on either cheek, he knows how to use his charms to get anything he wants.

"There's a lot that's happened between Ryder and me that I feel responsible for. Although," he says, setting his mug down to get a refill, "this isn't me fucking with you, little sister, this is me wanting what's best for him."

"And you think that's me?" This time I sound incredulous because I can't believe my brother would feel this way. Not that he's done much for me in the past. But this is a new side to him I never saw coming.

"Look, Pip." He turns to me, sipping his

drink before continuing. "All I'm saying is, give him a chance to explain. He's… volatile right now. And he needs someone to ground him."

Folding my arms in front of my chest, I regard him warily. "Fine, I'll go talk to him, but this"—I motion between us—"doesn't make anything that happened between us right."

"You're old enough to know people make mistakes." His response is confident. "At twenty you're practically a grown-up."

To that I laugh. "Well, Mom and Dad wouldn't agree," I tell him bitterly. I know they'll be home from the business trip tomorrow and I still have to broach the subject of me moving to the city.

"Let me handle them and you handle my best friend." Preston waggles his eyebrows and chuckles when I swat his shoulder.

"Don't be gross, Pres," I grumble and wrinkle my nose more in embarrassment than anything else. My cheeks heat when he offers me a wink.

He leaves me in the kitchen mulling over what he's told me. If something happened to Ryder and he's hiding behind some wall he's built, it won't be good once he finally breaks down. That's one thing about him. He's kept his pain inside and offered up a mask for as long as I've known him.

With every moment we've spent together, he thawed, but only for me. Perhaps my brother is right. Maybe I'm the only one who can get through to Ryder. I fill my mug with coffee and head back to my bedroom.

Finding my phone, I unlock the screen and scroll down to the number that's taunted me for months, years, and I finally hit dial on it. After talking to him only a few days ago, I feel less nervous when I hear the ringing on the other end. I recall being a teenager with a crush on my brother's best friend.

Even though he wasn't allowed in our house, not until much later just before they all headed off to college, I would always find a way to be around him, even if I didn't utter a word. I was in his orbit and that's all that mattered to me. My parents hated his appearance, he didn't fit in with their perfectly structured world. But Preston was never one to follow the rules. And Ryder became one of the trio along with Jeremiah. The three guys spent all their time together.

When his voicemail picks up my call, I drop my phone on the bed and head to my closet. Pulling out a pair of jean shorts and a tank top, I quickly pull them on. Thankfully my early morning shower has left me ready to walk out the door. If Ryder is depressed, if something is bothering him, then I need to get to him.

Once I've slipped my socked feet into my sneakers, I leave my forgotten coffee on the bedside table and race out the door with my phone in my pocket and keys in hand. I easily slip into the driver's seat of the small Mini Cooper my Dad insisted on buying me when I got my driver's license and I make my way to the warehouse.

There's no need to second-guess myself. I know he'll be there. And after our reunion two days ago at the same place, that's exactly where I'll find him.

The drive there is only ten minutes, but during that time, I doubt my choice to come here, to see him. I try to talk myself out of pushing Ryder to give me the truth, to explain what happened to him, but as I pull up to the warehouse and see his car parked near the entrance, my heart thrums wildly like the beat of a song in my chest. A melody only Ryder knows. And I know he needs me now, just as I needed him all my life.

He walked out.

It's my choice to walk back in.

EIGHT

RYDER

Solace.

Music.

Passion.

Three things that have kept me going. Even after all this time, I still find my happiness in the beats of a song. Even though I'm broken, I still have this one thing that allows me to remember who I am.

My life hasn't been easy. Yeah, I grew up wealthy, with friends in the same circle, fancy parties every weekend, but those things never made me happy.

Her face flits through my mind. As always,

I growl out my frustration as I listen to the beat, making up the moves as I do.

She's been a part of me for far too long. The young girl who didn't fit in, beside the boy who always stood out. When I went out with Preston and Jeremiah, people would stare. With my ink, my piercings, they thought I was trouble.

If only they knew.

And even then, when I was thought of as the bad boy in town, *she* saw me. Her big, innocent eyes looked through me, noticing the small parts of me I hid behind a tough exterior. It was Piper who gave me something to live for. She made me love when I believed I was incapable of loving. But I couldn't do much about my feelings for her, because she was far too young.

She's in the pool. I'm lying back on the lounger beside her brother. My eyes are glued to her behind my shades. Thankfully, Preston hasn't noticed me checking out his sister. Dressed in the skimpiest bikini known to man, she wades through the clear blue water and steps out of the pool.

Water trickles over her golden skin. The tight pink material hugs the globes of her ass. Small triangles cover what I want to see, what my mouth waters to devour. But I shake it off when I feel my groin churn with want.

Her hair, the color of silky spun gold, hangs down to the curve of her lower back, just above the waistline of her bikini bottoms. Long lithe legs—toned from her love of dancing—tease me.

"Dude," Preston grunts from beside me, jolting me up from where I've been ogling Piper.

"What?"

He sits up, handing me his phone. "Those two chicks invited us to their house party this weekend," he boasts, but I don't care. They don't hold my interest, but I can't tell him that, so I nod. "You coming?"

"Yeah, I'll be there."

He chuckles. Grabbing the device, he rises and presses it to his ear. "Hey, baby."

I turn back to Piper. She's dried off, but her hair is still dripping down her back. With a quick glance at Preston, I quickly make my way over to her. "You been practicing?" I question when I reach her as she strolls into the pool house. Her ass wiggles as she walks. Her hips sway hypnotically, and I'm entranced.

"Yeah, but I've hurt my ankle," she pouts and it takes all my restraint not to imagine what her mouth could do to me.

"Want me to check it out?" I offer, meeting her inquisitive stare.

"Okay." This time, she blushes. The rosy color looks good on her cheeks. She settles in the armchair, lifting her foot and placing it on my knee as I crouch down before her. My gaze immediately falls to the juncture between her thighs and my dick throbs. Shit.

Dragging my eyes away, I focus on her ankle. My fingers work the joint, causing soft whimpers to tumble from her lips, and I'm hard. Rock fucking hard. This was not a good idea. Shoving her leg away, I grit out through clenched teeth, "I have to go," and make my way out of the small living room, leaving her boring a hole in my back with her big blue eyes.

The memory of that day hangs over me like a storm cloud. Reminding me of what I had, how much that day changed me because that was the moment I knew I was in love with her. She followed me out of the pool house and told me she liked me.

"Ryder." Her voice stalls me mid-stride. "I saw... I mean... You back there," she stumbles over her words, but I can't face her because she'll see the bulge in my shorts. I'm not sure where her brother is, but I'm sure as shit glad he isn't out here.

"You don't know what you're talking about," I respond icily.

"Look at me," she demands this time. Feisty little girl. I give her what she wants. I turn to her. "I like you, Ryder. It's clear. Isn't it?"

"You shouldn't."

"Well, shit, it's not like I have a choice."

"Watch your mouth," I grit through clenched teeth, trying to imagine how hot it would be to hear her say fuck, to hear her moan my name.

"Why don't you watch it?" Her retort is spat hotly and I grip her chin between my thumb and forefinger, tugging her closer just with the simple touch. I lean in—praying to all the gods that her brother doesn't walk outside—and crash my mouth down on hers.

Her soft lips yield to mine easily. Her tongue—tentative and shy—darts out, tasting mine, and I can't help groaning at the sensation. She gently sucks my tongue into her mouth. The heat of her, the sweet taste of her innocence is enough to turn a *sane man crazy.*

It's enough to have me addicted, and I'm afraid that even if I pull away now, even if I never kissed her at all, I've been hooked for far longer than I care to admit.

I pull away, leaving her breathing heavily, and race into the house. In the bathroom, I shut the door and open the tap, splashing cold water on my face to keep from going back out there and taking her in front of the world. To lay claim to a pretty young girl who's fucked with my head.

The music that spills out of the speaker carries me through the movements. I try to shake Piper from my mind and focus on the dance. It's all fluid. My body curls and bounces through the routine I'm planning for the kids. There's a dance competition coming up in three weeks, and I need them to practice every day. This is their chance at finding solace in something that's always offered me happiness.

To find passion for something that will one day be something that could carry them into dance school.

School has always been important to me, and being able to help others follow their dream is something I want to do. Not being able to follow mine any longer still leaves a sour taste in my mouth, but I swallow it down as I think about their bright futures.

My body aches.

Everything hurts as sweat trickles down my back. I've been practicing for two days straight. But if I'm completely honest with myself, I've been avoiding Piper. After our talk the other night, I felt myself wanting her again, more so than I should allow myself, and that in itself is dangerous.

I pick up the pack of cigarettes on the speaker and tap one out. Flicking the lid of my Zippo, I light the white stick. Smoke fills my lungs and I breathe it in, the calm, the nicotine that offers me a serenity that alcohol can no longer do.

Every inch of me burns. There's tension in my muscles from the pain I live with daily. Both physical and emotional. I never should've come back. Seeing Piper again has done something to me. It's the same as it's always been with her. The more I see, touch, taste, the more I want and need.

Her light has always brightened my dark. She was perfect to all my flaws and even now, all grown up, she's still everything I need but also everything I can't have.

"You're here." Her voice comes from behind me, shocking me still. I turn to find Piper staring at me.

NINE
PIPER

"I am," he responds. There's a sheen of sweat on his toned upper body. His muscles are lean, but they're peaks and valleys of smooth tanned skin. The sweatpants he's wearing hang low on his tapered waist. The smooth line of V muscles points toward his groin.

A thin smattering of hair sits just below his belly button, along with a tattoo. The script font trails from left to right with the words *Perfectly Flawed* in dark ink. I can't tear my eyes away from the boy I recognize, who's turned into a man over the years.

"What are you doing here?" he asks,

toweling his chest as he regards me with a penetrating stare. I open my mouth, but I can't find the words. He's meant to be helping me with the dance competition, but all I want to do is leap into his arms. Work doesn't mean anything at this moment. "Butterfly?"

"I-I…" Clearing my throat, I try again. "I needed to talk to you about the choreography."

He nods, throwing the towel over one bare shoulder. There's a slight limp when he steps toward me and I don't miss the flinch on his handsome face. "What's wrong?"

"Nothing," he bites out. "I'll be at the school in an hour. I needed some time on my own. Get the kids ready for class and I'll take it from there."

"Ryder, you can't just walk in—"

"Do you want my help or not?" His tone is harsh, ragged, but there's anger that drips from each word.

"What happened to you?" I shake my head

as I voice the words.

"I grew up, Piper. I'm no longer the boy you had a crush on," he bites back in a tone I don't recognize. He's right, he's not the boy I remember. He's far from it. At this moment, he's a very angry man and there are ghosts in his eyes. Guilt perhaps.

"I can see you've turned into an asshole. You know, Ryder, with all that bravado you used to carry around, I don't see any of it now. What happened? Did some girl break your heart in LA? Huh?" I can't help myself. I'm prodding a sleeping bear and I know I'm only going to get bitten.

"Get out!" The demand he spits at me booms through the space like a foghorn, and when I meet those eyes I used to get lost in, I no longer recognize the person before me. The boy I fell in love with is gone, and he's been replaced by a shell of the man he once was.

"Fuck you, Ryder Kingsley!" My words

seem to shock him, as if I'd slapped him. "You're a pathetic asshole. Whatever happened to you does not give you the right to talk to me like that."

I spin on my heel, not bothering to stop when he calls to me. My name on his lips grips my heart, and the tether that's always been there threatens to pull me back. It makes me want to turn around and run back to him, but I don't.

Instead, I walk to the door and leave him in the godforsaken warehouse.

It's only when I slip into the driver's seat of my car that I blink, allowing the tears to fall. It's been a long while since I cried, really cried. My body wracks with silent sobs as I try to pull in air between the sadness that's taken over me.

The click of my door has my gaze snapping up to find Ryder standing at my car. The guilt painted on his expression is clear. There's something in his eyes, hidden to the world, but only visible to me, pure agony.

"Get out of the car." His voice is low, demanding. But I'm far too angry with him just to allow him to talk to me like that.

"Leave me alone, Ryder. I can't do this with you." Even though I'm twenty, he still makes me feel like the silly teenage girl who crushed on him all her life. It's stupid. I shouldn't let him get to me, but I can't stop my heart from thudding when he reaches into the car, his strong hand gripping my arm and pulling me from the seat.

"I said, get out of the car," he bites out, shoving my door closed and pressing me against the vehicle. "I've got so much darkness that seems to follow me around like a fucking storm, Piper." His words caress my skin, his hands holding my hips in place. His body is flush against mine, holding me in place.

I lift my gaze to meet his to see what he's hiding, but as much as I implore with a mere glance, I don't find the answers and he doesn't give them away. He's always been closed off. Even though my brother would get him drunk and take him to parties, I knew the real Ryder. The one who hid in the shadows because he was seen as a kid with no future.

"I can't drag you into my fucked up existence," he finally tells me. Allowing his pain to drip from every word, he crushes my heart with just that sentence alone.

"I've been in your fucked up existence for far longer than you believe, Ryder. I can't stop myself from loving you." My confession shouldn't be a problem. It shouldn't have him staring at me in shock.

"How can you love me, Piper?"

"I just never stopped," I inform him. And that's when I see them, the walls he's built up over the years he's been away. They're crumbling, and when he looks at me again, I see the agony that's so blatantly shining in his eyes.

"I'm not the same boy, not anymore. I'm not even a man."

TEN
RYDER

She stares at me, her big eyes wide with confusion. There's so much tension between us, it's stifling and I find it hard to breathe. I expect her to slap me, to do something, but she merely reaches for my face. Her soft hand cups my cheek.

"What broke you?" she finally questions.

Our eyes lock on each other and I don't know how to tell her, how to confess how much I fucked up.

"Life."

"That's a lie because when you left you were—"

"I was a boy who thought he owned the world, Piper," I tell her as much of the truth as I can muster. Turning away from her, I already miss the heat of her touch. "I was stubborn, carefree, and I thought everyone owed me something because of where I came from."

"That wasn't who you were," she argues.

"You only thought that because you were in love with me," I bite back, spinning on my heel to meet her fiery gaze.

"Fuck you, Ryder. I thought that because I knew the real you. I saw beneath that fucking asshole façade you put on for everyone." Piper takes a step toward me. Her eyes burn through me, begging and pleading for answers I cannot give her. It's in that moment that I know I love her. I'll always love her, but there's no way I can give her what she needs. What she deserves.

"It's time for you to leave. I'll be in class tomorrow to go over the routine."

She doesn't respond this time. I don't get

her voice when I need it. Right there, in those few seconds it takes her to nod and turn away from me, I feel it, the grip she has on my heart, on my soul. Piper slips into the car without a word. It squeezes the breath from me, and the pain I'd lived through the years I was away is nothing compared to watching the woman I love drive away from me.

I've finally fucked up everything in my life. Not only my dance career, but the only person who ever saw me for who I really am, just a broken little boy needing love.

Sighing, I run my fingers through my hair and tug hard at the strands. A bite of pain causes me to growl in response. *Why do I always do this?* Mess up everything I ever want.

"Dude," Preston's voice comes from behind me. I turn to find him sauntering toward me. His silhouette shadowed by the dimly lit warehouse. "Was that my sister in her car crying?"

"Yeah," I tell him honestly. I can't lie to my best friend. As much as he's an asshole at the best of times, he's also been there for me all my life. Given me an out, a chance.

"Did you tell her?"

"No," I grunt, grinding my teeth almost painfully. There's nothing I can do now because he won't stop until I've finally told her the truth.

"Why?"

"Because she deserves better than me," I tell him, meeting his incredulous stare. "I can't be the man for her."

"How do you figure that out, asshole?"

"You know why." I make my way into the warehouse without looking at him. The silent footfalls of his shoes are behind me as he follows and I know I'm in for a talk from my best friend.

"She loves you, Ryder. She's not going to walk away because of your past mistakes," he tells me earnestly. "Look, I never wanted you with her when we were at school because you were an asshole." He chuckles at my expression. "But she's an adult now, and you're more responsible than you have ever been. I know you love her. I'm not fucking blind."

Slumping against the table behind me, I watch my best friend stare at me. We're at a standoff and I know I'll lose. Preston is as stubborn as I used to be, but then again, I'm still as pigheaded as I've always been. Only now, I know I'm not worthy of the love Piper has given me and continues to give me.

"She's not going to give up."

"Stubbornness runs in the family then," I retort, causing him to chuckle and shake his head. His eyes burn into me with a warning I can't ignore. I know I have to tell her, but it scares the shit out of me.

"It does, and as you know, my sister is persistent." Preston stalks closer to me then.

He grips my shoulder, offering it a squeeze. "Don't hurt her, Ryder. Don't fucking hurt her."

He leaves me then, with that one warning. I don't need another, and I certainly do not need to know what he'll do to me if I do make her cry.

It's time to swallow my pride and come clean. I know it is. I turn to the stereo and find our song. My girl's song—"Good for You" by Selena Gomez. The beat takes me away and I move through the space like I used to.

Ignoring the way my body doesn't do the things I used to be able to do, I flow into the routine, popping over onto my hands, spinning around, my eyes closed in concentration as I recall her smile, her taste, her kiss. Those smooth, delicate hands that seem to touch me in a way that was both intimate and erotic. That makes my body come alive, just for her. No other girl could ever come close to Piper. No one else could make me feel like a man who was loved and appreciated, even though I was never worthy of her.

The movements are easy enough for the kids to pick up, and it allows me to practice with them without showing anyone how broken I really am. As soon as the song ends, I flip onto my feet and find my footing on the cold concrete floor.

"It's time for you to learn who you love, Butterfly," I tell the silence that surrounds me. "It's time for you to see who I've become."

ELEVEN

PIPER

My legs ache from the hours spent on the floor today. The beat of the song vibrates through me as I watch the routine Ryder has worked out for them. The song itself is one of my favorites, and I wonder if he chose it because of that.

All the years I've known him, he was always considerate and now as I watch him help one of the little girls to get her steps, my heart swells with pride at the man before me. Over the past few weeks, he's given me whiplash with his back and forth, but here, right in this moment, he's *my* Ryder. The boy

I fell for.

The kids are overly excited. Watching Ryder with them makes me smile. It's been so long since I saw him laugh, that as he leans in and whispers something in a little girl's ear and she starts giggling, it warms my heart.

After I left him last night, I went home to cry. I haven't done that in years, not since the day he left. But today, there's something about him that seems to have shifted. As if there's more of the old Ryder inside his eyes.

I enjoy the moment. Just looking at him. Seeing the boy who walked out so many years ago and broke my heart, I smile because even though it hurt, he's back. And if it's the last thing I do, I'm going to make him see that he is worthy of having happiness in his life, even if he doesn't choose me.

I've always been afraid. Scared he would come home with another girl on his arm, someone smarter than me, prettier, or just someone who wasn't me. But he didn't, and that gives me hope that perhaps my love for him was strong enough to bring him home to me.

There's no clue as to what he feels for me anymore. Yes, when I was far too young, he cared for me. But that was a long time ago. Now I may just be the little sister of his best friend, but when Ryder's gaze falls on me, I'm sure there's much more to it.

More emotion.

More secrets hidden in those depths.

And most of all, I can see he still cares.

"That's it for today, kiddos." He smiles, receiving a loud *Ahhhhh* in response. He's a natural with them, and they love him. As much as he taught and danced with them, though, I notice the way he took it easy on his moves. From what I remembered, Ryder was always the one to go overboard, enjoying himself to the music, this was very different. And I noticed it in the warehouse as well.

He makes his way over to me as soon as we're alone, settling on the small footstool opposite me. His top is cut out beneath the arms, showing off his toned, cut torso. Deep golden skin greets me as he moves and I can't help taking in the colorful patterns and drawings on his arms.

His ink has always been my weakness. The piercings in his nipples were always intriguing because ever since I saw them, I wanted to flick my tongue over them to see how sensitive each one was.

"You okay?" His voice cuts through the dirty thoughts, causing me to blush. The heat on my cheeks gives away my embarrassment.

"Yeah, you looked good with them," I tell him, meeting his gaze, trying to find where he goes to when we're alone.

The tension in his shoulders tells me something is coming. And I'm not sure I'm ready for it just yet. I don't think I'll ever be prepared.

"Are you leaving after this?" I question, wanting to get it out before he tells me goodbye, before he takes my heart and breaks it again.

Ryder stares at me for a moment before he looks away. He doesn't respond, and the silence is heavy in the room after all the noise and laughter from just moments ago. The music is no longer playing, and all I can hear are his deep breaths.

"Look, you don't have to stay. I just—"

"There's something I need to tell you, to show you," he finally says, snapping his dark stare to mine. They flit left to right, as if he's trying to see into my heart, searching for my soul that's buried so deep in the rubble of our past. All the pain he left me with is still there, a site of destruction where my love for him still fights every day.

"Then show me, Ryder. Give me

something," I finally beg. All my life I've been stubborn, closing myself to emotion, but Ryder was the only one who managed to break through my high teenage walls, find my young, innocent heart, and fill it with the first love I'd ever known. But he also took that love and walked out.

He shifts on the chair. Leaning in closer, he murmurs, "Come to my place."

"What?"

"What I have to tell you and show you, I'd rather do it in private. It's not easy for me to talk about." The anguish on his face, in his expression, tells me this isn't some booty call. There's something dark in his eyes, and my heart aches at what I'm about to learn about the first boy I'd ever loved, the only boy I'll ever love.

TWELVE
RYDER

She nods, "Okay," and my heart ceases to beat for a moment. I need to calm the fuck down. It's time and I need to man up. Grow some balls as Preston would say.

"I'll drive," I tell her, rising from the chair, not giving her a chance to respond. My keys jingle in my hand as I grab her rucksack.

"I just need to turn the lights off and lock up." Her voice quivers. I notice it immediately. She's nervous. So am I.

"Okay."

Once we're in the car, she stares at me for a moment before smiling. "You really did look good with the kids."

"They're good."

I turn on the stereo, flicking through songs before I find the one I want and pull out onto the road. I can feel her eyes on me, burning through me with questions I can't answer just yet. It's been a long time since I did this, confessed what I am to someone. But then again, the last time I did, it was only Preston. There wasn't anything more he could say because he was there, he knew before I told him.

Anxiety riddles through me, eating away at the strength I've been mustering up to tell Piper. It feels as if we'll never get to my place as I weave through the early evening traffic.

"So," she starts as we pull up to a red light. "Did you ever think of me when you were away?"

Her question squeezes my heart. My chest painfully tightens when I realize the one time I didn't think about her was when I got into the car that night and I had my arm hanging around the shoulders of a stranger. It lasted for a good ten minutes. Those moments play over and over in my mind, and I regret every fucking second of it.

"Piper—"

"No, you know what, don't tell me. I just... I don't know. I just feel like the stupid teenager who believed your promises."

I pull away from the light, gripping the steering wheel because I want to shout at her. I want to tell her I love her. To tell her that every moment I was away, bar those few, she was the only person I wanted and needed. To explain that my love for her never fizzled out, it never wavered.

To tell her that even though I had fucked another girl before I met her, she is the only one I will ever want, now and forever. But before I can tell her that and confess my feelings, I need her to see me.

"You're not stupid, Piper."

"Am I not?" she questions quietly, her voice so low, so sad that it knocks the breath from my lungs. I did this. I made her feel so wary because I took all the love she gave me and I didn't give her anything in return.

"No," I bite out, casting a quick, furious glance her way. "Fuck, Piper, can you quit with the shit until we get to my place because I can't focus on the road when you're spewing bullshit."

"You're angry, but not at me," she observes and she's right. I'm angry at myself for hurting her all those years ago when I should've laid my fucking claim on her, but she was too young. Far too young and innocent for me. But what makes it so different now?

"I am angry, because I fucked up with you," I tell her, my stare glued to the road because I can't meet those inquisitive eyes.

The song changes, and "Echo" by Jason

Walker starts and I know this is not the type of song I need right now. That *we* need right now. I reach over to change it, but her delicate hand is on mine in an instant.

"Leave it."

"Piper—"

"Listen to it, Ryder," she pleads and I can't deny her anything, so I do. By the time I pull up to the apartment complex, the song ends and I park in my designated spot. Not moving, I stare out of the window, waiting for her to say something, but she sits beside me in silence.

I push the door open and round the back, tugging her door open. I offer her my hand, which she takes. I lead her into the building, into the elevator, still holding on to her hand as if she's a lifeline and I'm caught in a raging storm.

The ding startles me and the doors slide open, spitting us out into the hallway, and I turn left toward the door. Unlocking it quickly,

I release Piper's hand, feeling the loss of her the moment the contact is gone.

"Make yourself at home," I tell her, following in behind my sweet girl. Because that's what she is. Mine. She's always been mine. Since the moment I laid my eyes on her, I knew there was no other woman for me.

THIRTEEN
PIPER

I settle on the sofa that looks like it's seen better days, but it's comfortable. The cushions are a deep purple, reminding me of the first pair of sneakers I got from my folks when I started dancing. The soles illuminated in the dark and looked amazing when I would drop to my hands and spin my feet in the air. Ryder loved them, so I did too.

"Get out of your pretty little head, Butterfly," he says, his voice thick and heavy with emotion. His eyes—the deep green more prominent in this moment than the hazel—make them look like a darkened forest.

"I'm here." I smile up at him, watching him move through the space and head into what I'm guessing is the kitchen.

"Do you want a drink?" he questions from the other room.

I push off the sofa and follow him into a spacious kitchen, which is empty except for the breakfast bar that separates the eating area from the work space.

"What have you got?" I ask, stepping up behind him, the heat of his body so close that I want to melt into it, into him.

"Coke, Pepsi, water, or orange juice." He lifts the carton to his nose, giving it a sniff. He scrunches his nose, causing me to giggle. "Okay, I don't have orange juice."

"Coke is fine," I tell him.

Ryder grabs a glass, pops the can open, and fills the tumbler with the dark, fizzy liquid. He pours himself one as well, and we head back into the living room.

Once I'm on the sofa, he takes the seat to my right, and the earlier lightheartedness is gone. Right now, we've reached the tension again, and I don't know what's coming. All I can tell is that it's something terrible.

"I spent so long wondering how I'd ever tell you what I did, that now that we're finally here I don't have a speech mapped out. I haven't planned the words, so you'll have to bear with me. I haven't spoken about it in a long time."

"Ryder, this is me you're talking to. I'll never judge you for being young and stupid." I smile, hoping it will earn me his usual dimpled grin, but it doesn't. Instead, his eyes meet mine and I know there'll be no smiles tonight.

"I know, Piper, I know." He sighs. Leaning forward, he places his elbows on his thighs, then meets my gaze. "I was out partying one night. Your brother wanted to drive, but I didn't want him to since he'd been drinking more than I had. He was being stubborn, so

I took his keys and..." His voice drops lower, and I find myself glued to his every word. "I had just spoken to my father that day. He told me he was cutting me off completely, so I had a few beers during the day. That night, I had one at the party and planned to get wasted."

"Why was your dad cutting you off?"

"He wasn't happy with me for some reason. He didn't need to explain. It was just how our relationship worked. He was disappointed in me and I didn't give a shit. I'd been drinking a lot over those few weeks, more than usual."

The guilt that drips off his every word has my body trembling, and I have a feeling he's going to break me with his confession.

"I got behind the wheel that night after I'd had a few too many. There was a girl beside me. Your brother and his girlfriend were in the back seat."

I attempt to swallow past the lump in my throat, from what he's telling me, to the fact that jealousy has reared its head. He was with another girl. He was partying and getting drunk. He was enjoying his life.

"Stop." His command has me snapping my attention back to him. His eyes are hard on me. "She was a girl I offered a lift to, nothing more."

"I didn't—"

"Piper, I know you. I can see the wheels turning in your head."

Shrugging it off, I lift my drink and gulp down the rest of my Coke. He doesn't speak until I've set the glass on the table.

"I didn't see the other asshole coming toward me." The words feel surreal, as if they're told to me and I'm on the other side of a thick window. Muffled. Ringing in my ears deafening me at the next few words. "I swerved, but it was too late. The car rolled. I don't know how many times. No one was killed, thankfully, but—"

"Ryder—"

He doesn't say anything. Instead, he rises, and I watch as he moves, in slow motion. The hiss of the zipper of his hoodie is so loud I want to scuttle backward from the noise. His fingers deftly untie the string of his sweatpants. Then he eases the gray material down his muscled thighs.

"This is the so-called man you want to love," he tells me sadly when I take in a blurry glance at the mechanical part of Ryder where half of his left leg used to be. From the knee down, there's nothing but plastic and metal. Or something. I don't even know.

I open my mouth to respond. To tell him I love him. But I can't. No words form on my tongue, but they all sit like a poison, venomous in their attack on my system. On my mind.

"I fucked up that night. I hurt people because of my own stupidity, Piper. That's not someone you want in your life. I'm no fucking man to give you a life."

He covers himself, jerking his sweatpants up, he leaves me in the living room. I'm staring at nothing because he's no longer standing in the spot he vacated, where my eyes are glued to. Tears drip from my chin, my body wracks with sobs. Not because he's *not* the man I want, but because he's so much more.

He is perfectly flawed.

FOURTEEN
RYDER

I walked out. I fucking left her in my living room after showing her what I've been living with for two long years. The reason I can't be with her. Not because I think she can't love me the way I am, but because I can't love me the way I am.

I don't hear movement from the other room. She's either still in shock or so disgusted with me, she can't look me in the face. Scrubbing my hands over my face, I feel the frustration ebbing through me, flowing over every part of me. I know I had to do it, tell her the truth, but nothing could've prepared me for the way she watched me so silently.

Piper has always been feisty, sassy. Seeing her still in silence is something new that has my anxiety hitting hard, slamming into me. My head is still in my hands when a tentative knock on the door drags my attention to the entrance of my bedroom.

"Hey." She smiles. Her sweetness is what I've always craved. The gentleness she possesses is so different from my harshness. Her light to my dark.

"Hey."

"Can we talk?" She steps farther into the room, and her perfume wafts around me. The sweet scent of apples, reminding me of dessert. Of sweetness and happiness. As if it's her own fragrance and no one else can wear it because no other woman I've been near has ever smelled like Piper.

"Yeah, sure."

I don't know what she's going to say, or

do, but she settles beside me on the mattress, not touching, but close enough for me to feel her heat. It's as if there's an electrical current traveling through me at her nearness. It's always felt like this with her. As if I *need* to touch her. That if I didn't, I wouldn't be able to breathe.

"I was shocked back there," she starts, gesturing to the living room with her small, delicate hand. "I'm so sorry you lived through that alone."

"I wasn't—"

"Let me finish." Her eyes blaze, meeting mine in a standoff.

Lifting my hand, I gesture for her to continue. That's another thing about her. She's stubborn. She won't listen to me if I tried to stop her now. Once she's got her head set on something, the girl is relentless. I learned that a long time ago, and it's just one of the things I love about her.

"I wish I'd been there for you. I know it's stupid, but I wish I'd been the one beside you in the car because I would've stood right beside you as you healed, Ryder." She says my name with so much love that it hits me hard in the chest making it difficult to breathe. "I love you. You may not think you're worthy of me, or whatever the hell you think, but you're wrong."

"Piper, I—"

She rises, her hands on her hips as she glares me into silence. "Ryder, I never had a choice in my feelings for you. From the moment we met, there was something between us. Granted, I was far too young, but I knew I'd love you." She sounds so sure, so confident in what she felt.

"You were too young, Piper. I kissed you and I shouldn't have," I tell her. "I should've been responsible, but all those times I looked at you, at your mouth, your eyes, everything about you, I knew I could never be the man who gives you what you want."

"What *do* I want?" She folds her arms across her chest, her gaze blazing wildly in a challenge. She's baiting me to see what I'll say and somehow I think every answer I come up with will be wrong.

"You want a forever. You deserve a forever."

"Why don't you let me decide what I want?" This time, she places her hands on my chest, shoving me backward onto the bed. The sprite crawls up over me, her thighs on either side of my hips, and once more, her heat is right at my crotch, making it difficult to think straight. "I've waited for you, Ryder. For four long years I waited. And now," she says, leaning in to nip at my neck, her lips sucking the flesh into her hot mouth, causing a groan to rumble deep in my throat. "Now all I want is this," she whimpers, rolling her hips against my ever growing hard-on.

"Piper—"

"You made a promise to me, Ryder," she moans, kissing my neck, trailing her way over the scruff on my jaw as she reaches my mouth.

Our lips hovering inches apart, if I lift my head, I'll kiss her. *Do I follow the rules I set for myself? Or do I claim the girl who's always owned me?*

FIFTEEN
PIPER

"You've never been good at lying, at self-control, or looking at me and not wanting me," I tell him. Honesty is raw in my words. The heat of his breath fans over me, making me needier than I've ever felt. There's no denying that we've always been like magnets. We need each other to be whole. Two halves of the same soul, and even though our hearts have been broken, those pieces always fit together perfectly. My sadness and pain from never being good enough for my mother, and Ryder's pain from being judged unfairly all his life.

"Piper," he growls my name, reaching for

my long blond hair, tugging the ponytail back, exposing my neck to him. "You're a fucking temptation." He grits out through clenched teeth, his lips feathering over the sensitive skin that's now dotted with goosebumps from his warm breath.

I can't help smiling at his confession. "Wasn't I always?"

"Since the moment I laid my eyes on you, Butterfly," he murmurs before his lips find mine. It's not rough, nowhere near what I thought it would be. No. This is Ryder being gentle, and the kiss itself sears me.

He pulls me closer. His tongue darts out, licking at my lips, causing me to whimper. My hips undulate as I press myself closer to him, needing him nearer, so impossibly close that it's like he's a part of me. And he is. Always has been.

His other hand grips my hip, fingers digging into the flesh, holding me still. When he pulls away, his gaze meets mine, burning through me.

"We can't do this right now," he tells me earnestly.

"Why?"

"I… We need time."

Sighing, I go to move off him, but he holds me steady. "If you don't want me then—"

"It's not that, Piper." Frustration is evident in his voice, thick and heavy with emotion. "I've just shown you what I did, who I am."

"I know." I reach up, placing my hands on either side of his face. The stubble tickling my palms, the heat of him warming me, keeping me lit up like a fire raging through the forest. "But you've also given me so much more," I tell him. "You've given me your fear, your pain, your guilt."

"I never wanted you to have those things. I've just wanted love and happiness for you." He tries to look away, but I hold him close, keeping his eyes on mine. I want him to see my love, the love I've held for him all my life. Since the moment I met Ryder I knew, and I've always known that no matter what tries to come between us, we'll weather the storm.

"I have love and more happiness than you can imagine, and I have it because I have you here." He stares at me for a moment as if he can't fathom what I'm saying. It's as if each word doesn't make sense to him.

His sigh is low. His chest rises and falls. It's then that I lean in, burying my face in his neck, inhaling the scent of Ryder. Masculine with a hint of mint and Coke. Suddenly, he tugs me, lifting me against him, and placing me on the mattress.

"Stay."

I watch as he takes his shoes off. The movements are jerky, and I wonder if it hurts. My eyes are glued to him and the moment he finally pushes the pants he's wearing down,

I'm met once more with the fact that Ryder is missing a leg. "I didn't want you to ever see this," he tells me with his back to me. "To see me broken." There's so much sadness in his tone that makes my heart hurt, it physically aches in my chest.

"We're all somewhat broken, Ryder. Every person has a part of themselves missing. Just because yours is physical doesn't mean you're different from someone who's suffered or is suffering mentally or emotionally."

He turns to me then. "When did you grow up, baby girl?"

"When you weren't here." I murmur, but I don't say it to hurt him, or to make him feel guilty for going away. I need him to know I'm no longer the little girl he walked out on four years ago.

Ryder settles onto the side of the bed. Then I watch in wonderment as he places his prosthetic leg against the nightstand. It hits me all at once, he's lived with this for two years. All those months he was alone, hurting, coming to terms with the accident and what he did.

"I understand why you were angry."

He doesn't turn to me when I talk, but I know he can feel every word. We've always had a powerful connection. I didn't realize it until he left, and I felt like a part of me was missing.

"I'm not saying it's the same thing, but after you went to the city, it felt like I had a part of me missing. I couldn't function normally, for a long while. And it took months before I found my love of reading, of dancing again. I even started up with ballet again just to please my mother," I confess in a raspy tone that drips with sadness and pain.

He swings his legs onto the bed and pulls me into his arms without responding. The part of him no longer there doesn't scare me. It doesn't disgust me. It just makes me want to hold him even closer.

Our bodies press closely together. I can feel his erection against me, but I don't say anything about it because this moment isn't about that. It isn't about anything other than Ryder healing, about him letting go of years of pain and regret, of guilt and burden. And I allow him to hold me.

He nestles his head into my hair that's splayed on his pillow. Silence hangs around us, heavy and threatening. It feels as if there's a storm brewing in the distance—the clouds dark and menacing—and I have a feeling something is about to break free.

And then I feel it.

I feel him.

Ryder is crying.

And all I can do is hold him.

SIXTEEN
RYDER

Her body is warm. Calming. And as the emotional pain grips me, I let it all go as I inhale her scent. Her fragrance. Piper is the only thing I have ever needed in my life. She brought happiness where there was sadness, she brought light when I was drenched in darkness, and she filled me with love when I'd only ever hated.

Her hand gently trails its way up and down my back. Her body cocooned against mine is right where I want her to be. She doesn't speak. She allows me to cry. For the first time in two long years, I let the pent-up anger and guilt to free itself from me, and I cry.

The tears burn their way down my cheeks. Honesty and pain drip from my eyes as I hold on to the only woman to ever love me. And the love she offers isn't conditional. It doesn't matter who I am, what I look like. She'll be here.

"There were times over the four years I would wonder about you. I'd imagine you in a life so perfect, filled with dance and music, with love and beauty," Piper whispers. "Each time I saw you in my mind's eye, I smiled. Knowing you were happy was enough for me."

"I could never be happy without you." I lift my head, allowing my eyes to find Piper's big blue ones. "You're everything to me, Butterfly. Even when I was away I was still right here," I tell her, placing my index finger on her chest where her heart is beating wildly against my touch.

"And I was here," she tells me, mimicking

my movement by placing her fingers on my chest. Her leg moves, intertwining with mine. It's strange having a woman in bed with me. Knowing I'm missing half my limb is difficult, but sharing that with someone is even more so. "Will you tell me about your past?" she questions then.

"What about my past?" I have a feeling I know what she means, but I don't know if I can even tell her about that time of my life, the moment I learned my father was a cheating bastard. I didn't know the whole truth, but I overheard him and my mother fighting. He'd been with someone else and she found out somehow.

"Why did you... I mean, why..." Piper's voice is a raspy murmur, and I know what she's asking.

"For a long time, I felt alone. As an only child, I was nothing more than an inconvenience to two parents who didn't really want a child."

I reach for her, stroking her cheek as she watches me with those inquisitive orbs of blue. "They always told me I was an accident. After all those years of hearing it, I figured they'd be better off without me around."

Silence hangs around us, the room quiet in her pondering. She nods slowly, then speaks. "I get that. There were times when I thought that of my own family." Piper tells me something she's never mentioned before. "But then I found you. I found dance."

My gaze pierces her the same way her words stab me. "What?"

She smiles. "I guess you saved me."

We don't move. We can't. There's nothing more to say because we've all said it all before, not with words, but with actions.

"I want to dance with you," Piper says suddenly.

"What?"

"Like we did in the warehouse." My girl

is adamant and I know there's no way to dissuade her. Instead of saying no, I want to give her everything she wants.

I nod. "It was fun, but I don't think I can match you anymore," I tell her, noticing the sadness in my voice. I don't hide it, not anymore because she sees me. She knows who I am now, and she hasn't run away, she's stayed, and I feel like a man who's won the lottery.

"You don't need to match me, Ryder, you need to just be with me."

"I don't know how to do that anymore." My honesty burns my throat. I swallow the lump in my throat, attempting to find my voice once more. "I need you, Piper."

"I'm right here." She smiles, leaning her forehead against mine, then slowly snuggles her way into the crook of my neck and soon, I'm holding on to her, my arms wrapped around her small frame. Her legs against mine, against the part of me that's broken, and her soft, silky skin touches the part of me where they took my leg. The sensation is strange, feeling someone so close, so intimate.

I can't speak. My eyes burn as emotion grips my chest and breathing is difficult as I try to figure out how I'm going to keep this woman who deserves so much more than I can give her. Even though she's said she wants me, there's still a hint of doubt in my mind.

"Ryder." Piper's voice drags me from my thoughts. When I meet her big blue eyes, she's staring at me with a soft smile on her lips. "You're poking me." This time, there's a giggle that tumbles from her lips and I realize I'm hard.

"Shit, I'm sorry." I attempt to move away, but she holds on to me.

"It's okay. You were just... I mean you were," she says, gesturing with her hands. "Prodding my stomach."

A laugh falls from my lips, a real, honest to

goodness laugh, and I can't stop it.

Happiness isn't a place.

It isn't a feeling. It's a person.

It's Piper.

She's my happy place, my sanctuary and nothing will ever change that.

"Your brother told me not to hurt you," I tell her.

"He did?" She sounds surprised at my confession, which causes me to drag my gaze over to her. Her brows furrow and she looks like a pixie with a frown.

"He knows how I feel about you."

"Preston really has been acting really strange lately." Her observation is true. Her brother has been different since we've been back and I wonder what it could be about. He's always been an asshole, and even though he still is to a certain extent, him permitting me to talk to Piper was a shock to me.

I would never have guessed he'd ever

approve of his best friend with his baby sister. But Preston has seen me at my worst. He fucking survived the accident I caused, and even though I almost killed him, he's still my best friend.

"Are you thinking about it?"

I glance up at Piper, her question catching my attention and dragging me from the racing images that filter through my mind on a daily basis.

"Yes," I answer her honestly because that's what I can give her. My honesty. My truth.

"You know, living in the past is only an excuse for so long, Ryder." Her smile falls away and I know I'm in trouble now. "Soon you'll have to look forward and when you do, you'll regret missing out on so many good things because you were stuck in the past."

"You're still as fucking feisty as you always were," I tell her, reaching up to cup her face in my hands. Pulling her closer, I plant a chaste kiss on her plump lips. They're soft and taste like cola and cherries.

"Can we lie here forever?" Piper whispers against my mouth. Her soft breath fans over my face as she speaks and I want to pull her closer, to revel in her scent and sweetness. I want to climb inside of her and never leave.

"We can. But I think the outside world would be angry," I tell her.

"Why?" Her brows furrow. Her eyes sparkle with confusion as she regards me and I take a moment before I answer, because everything she does leaves me speechless.

"Because I would've stolen the sun from the sky."

"Okay, cheesy." She laughs, swatting my chest playfully, and I wrap my arms around her and snuggle into the soft comforter with her lying close.

"This is nice." I plant a kiss on her hair, the silky strands tickling my lips, but I want so much more of her. Soon. Not tonight. This moment is far too innocent to turn into something more. It's like coming home.

I never thought I'd ever feel that way about this place, but with her in my bed, beside me, it feels like the world is right. Like I'd always meant to come home. To her.

SEVENTEEN
PIPER

I'm startled awake by a door slamming against the wall. When my gaze snaps open, I find Jeremiah standing on the threshold of the bedroom staring at Ryder and me in bed, curled around each other like old lovers.

"Well, good morning to you two." He smiles, partly in shock, and the rest is in camaraderie at Ryder, whose arms are still tightly wrapped around me. "Does your brother know you're here?" he questions, meeting my gaze.

"No, but I'm an adult and I can be wherever I like." My confidence falters when Preston strolls into the bedroom behind his best friend.

"Pip." He nods, then saunters toward the desk, settling himself on the top. "Ryder," he starts, causing my heart to kick wildly in my chest. I know he told me to go after Ryder, after my heart, but seeing us in bed could make him change his mind. "Just remember one thing, you hurt her, I'll hurt you. And you won't enjoy it."

"Fuck off. Both of you, get out of my bedroom." At that, Ryder hurls a pillow at Preston, who catches it easily. I chuckle at the display of testosterone in the bedroom.

"We'll wait in the living room," Jeremiah informs us as he strolls out, along with my brother, who follows close behind.

Groaning, I push up, swinging my legs over the edge of the bed. "I better go."

"Like fuck you are. They'll be leaving soon. Wait here." Ryder moves quickly, putting on the prosthetic, and is on his feet in seconds and out in the living room. Their deep voices hurtle my way through the open doorway. "Can we get some alone time? I told her last night."

"As I said, I'm not angry, but don't fucking break her heart, man." My brother's warning to Ryder makes me smile. Growing up, we'd never been close, but I guess some things do change.

"You know I won't. Now get your ass out of here. I need to spend time with my lady." Ryder's gruff tone comes through loud and clear, causing me to laugh at his words.

"Man, you're whipped." Jeremiah chuckles.

I hear the door clicking, and then I'm sure we're alone. I don't leave his bedroom. I'm sitting on the bed when he finally makes his way back into the space carrying two large mugs of steaming coffee.

"Extra cream for you, little lady," he tells me with a smile that makes my heart skip a few extra beats. Ryder is handsome, in a rough, rugged way. And that was the reason I fell for him when I didn't even know what love was. He wasn't fake. He was real, honest. Nothing he said had that condescending tone some of the boys at school used to have. He treated me like an equal.

"Thanks."

"I would've made you breakfast in bed, but Jer and Preston interrupted us," he tells me, a smile on his lips that's almost shy. Unusual for Ryder.

"You know, you don't have to spoil me," I tell him, scooting closer to where he's perched on the edge of the mattress. "And I'm not going anywhere, so maybe we can spend the day in bed, talking."

"Butterfly, if we spend the day in bed, there will be no talking, unless it's you screaming my name over and over again for hours."

A giggle slips free from my lips then. I haven't genuinely laughed in so long. It feels foreign to me. He pulls me closer, and I let him. I needed this, and I just didn't realize how much I needed him. His arms are like a foundation, and my heart is clearly teetering on the ledge.

When Ryder left, I promised myself not to fall again. I also vowed that if he ever came back, I wouldn't let him drag me into his orbit, but there was no way I'd win that war. I couldn't fight the gravitational pull I have toward him, but there is nowhere else I'd rather be.

"I want to make you breakfast," he announces, pressing a kiss to my forehead like he used to when I was a teenager. "Do you still like choc chip pancakes?"

"Is that even a question?"

Ryder stands, tugging me off the bed and into his hold. I tilt my head to meet his gaze. "If you sass me again I may have to put you over my knee and give that pretty little ass a spank." His threat turns my insides to goo, and the butterflies he always seemed to awaken within me flurry to life.

"Is that a promise?" I tease, causing him to swat my ass. "Ouch!"

"It's a promise, Butterfly." He smirks. "Let's go make something to eat." Slipping his fingers through mine, he leads me into the modern kitchen, which looks like it's not been used. But then again, this is Ryder and I'm certain he's never cooked before.

He pulls out bowls, flour, eggs, salt, and some baking powder, along with two small packets of chocolate chips, and milk. I watch as Ryder moves around the kitchen, my coffee mug in front of me. There's nothing more I need than being here with him. I know that. I guess I've always known that.

"You seem to have the the right ingredients for pancakes," I observe when he sets everything out on the counter.

"It's my ritual. I make them because they

remind me of you," he tells me, not meeting my questioning gaze. He moves about the kitchen and I allow him to mix what he needs to before I voice the words that have been sitting on my tongue since last night.

"So, how long was your rehabilitation?" I whisper, unsure of how to start all the questions I have running around in my mind. There's a barrage of them and I feel like asking too many might give Ryder the opportunity to slip back into the darkness what still flickers in his eyes.

"It took months, over a year to finally accept it. There are still times I don't believe it," he tells me sadly. His voice is low, gravelly with emotion as he informs me about his past. The one I wasn't there for.

"Why didn't you come home?" I'm genuinely curious.

Ryder halts all movement. Slowly, he turns to face me. The expression on his face is pure agony and I'm afraid I've just messed up our bliss.

"Honestly?" he asks and I nod, my heart thumping wildly in my throat, making it difficult to swallow. "I didn't want you to see me like that, so broken."

"You're not broken, you never were," I tell him, rising to my feet and rounding the counter. "Even when you told me about your past, about what you did…" I allow my words to filter into the silence that surrounds us. For the first time in a long while, there's no music. It's only the rhythm of our hearts.

"Piper, you've only seen the parts of me you wanted to. The bad boy you had a crush on, he was the one you wanted," he tells me. He's so sure of himself.

"No, Ryder, that's not all I saw. Deep down, I saw those dark parts of you, that side you hide from everyone else. That's the Ryder I fell in love with. All those scared, lonely parts, along with the handsome, snarky parts. Don't make me sound like a stupid kid who has a crush." My frustration is evident in my words, and Ryder hears it.

Cupping my face in his hands, he pulls me closer, so his breath is mine. "I didn't mean it like that. I just meant…" He sighs gently. Then offers a wry smile. "When you love someone, you put them on a pedestal."

"Is that what you did to me?"

EIGHTEEN
RYDER

Her question stills me for a moment. No matter how I want to deny it, I can't. Yes, I did put Piper on a pedestal, but that's where she belongs.

"Don't stare at me like that," she quips, placing her hands on her hips. "I'm no saint."

"Oh?" I respond, my eyebrow arching in question. "Tell me, little Butterfly, what nasty things have you been doing?" I lean in, trailing my lips over the shell of her ear, allowing my warm breath to draw out a soft whimper from her. "Were you alone in your bed, dreaming about the big bad wolf? Did he climb through the window and devour you?"

Our banter has always been our foreplay. The back and forth we throw at each other is my weakness, because it takes all my restraint not to bend her over the worktop and lick her from her heels to her pert little backside.

"You don't play fair, at all, Ryder." She pouts. Her full pink lips make me lick my own. Leaning in, I plant a soft kiss on her mouth, and another, and another. With each moment of contact between us, heat scorches through me. We should get to the school to go through the routine, but I know a better place to take her.

"I'm taking you to the warehouse."

She pulls away, her eyes searching mine. "To dance?"

It's been so long since we've done a routine together, since I've just let myself feel the music. I nod. "Yes. We'll dance."

"Will we do it to a song of my choice?

You always promised to teach me something that's not conventional." The hope in her eyes holds me hostage, gripping me so hard I can't breathe. Since we met and she fell into my world, I promised her a routine. One I've long since forgotten.

"I'm not sure I can." It's an honest answer.

She nods. "I get it."

"But for you I'll try."

Tears shine in her eyes, making them glisten like two large orbs of see-through glass.

"I'll always try for you."

She leans up on her tiptoes, pressing her closed mouth on mine. The heat of her kiss taunts my barely there restraint.

"Now make me pancakes." She giggles as she steps back, settling herself on the stool. Shaking my head with a chuckle, I grab the bowl and start to mix the ingredients while she tells me about the kids she's been teaching.

When we reach the warehouse, it's empty, and this is why I love coming here. The silence that greets me each time is calming, especially when I needed to think and get away from the noise of my childhood home. This building was my sanctuary.

I still can't believe Piper recalls the day I told her about what I did. My weakness was evident that day, shining right through. I hated my life, my parents didn't understand who I was, but then again, what teenager believes their folks are there as a support rather than a hindrance.

Shoving the large metal door open, it creaks loudly in protest. I allow Piper to enter first. She wanted to stop at home to change before coming here. Seeing her in those low-hung gray sweatpants, the bright purple sports bra, and the blue tank top with large ripped sections on the front and back—that looks like it's seen better days—has me recalling the times I'd had to swallow down my desire for her.

At the time, she was far too young. I would've gone to jail. But now, all bets are off. She's twenty, old enough to make her own decisions, and adult enough for me to stare at and imagine her naked.

"Are you going to stand there all day staring at me?" she quips, pulling out her iPod, placing it on the docking station.

"Just appreciating the view, Butterfly," I tell her, stalking closer to the space we'd made a dance floor out of so many times before.

Before I have time to think, the song in question comes on, and I recognize it immediately. *That song.* It was released about a year ago, before I decided to walk back into her life. When I'd first heard it, I thought about working on a routine for it.

And this is certainly unconventional. Even though it's not your average hip hop song, the beat is there, and I can get the eight count for the steps.

"Shape of You" by Ed Sheeran always made me think of her. No matter where I was, what I was doing, I had to stop and remember her.

Each time I've heard it since, it's been like a shot to the heart, threatening to kill me.

"This is the song you wanted?" I question, nearing her as she turns to face me.

She smiles, shrugging before responding. "Yeah, you up for it, old man?"

"Don't sass me, Piper, you know I'll take you over my knee," I warn before pulling the hoodie I'm wearing off, chucking it on the chair beside the stereo.

"You have an idea for steps then, smartass?" she questions, arching her golden eyebrow at me.

"Come here, Butterfly that's soon to have a sore ass." I tug her over to the dance floor, placing her in front of me, my body cocooning hers as I grab her hips and hold her steady. I wait out the last few strings before the song replays.

Her breathing speeds up, but I grip her tightly.

"Remember your fifteenth birthday dance," I whisper in her ear and she nods. "Good girl, same count, same steps. And go." I release her and she flows into the drop, spinning on her knees to face me, grabbing my hand as I tug her from the floor.

The slim frame against mine has every nerve in my body electric. Reaching for her hips, I lift her into the air, turning as the beat drops. Her back arches like I taught her, her hands in the air, her legs high. She looks like a fucking beautiful swan in my hands.

"Now drop." My order comes swiftly and I allow her to slide down my front, her breasts squashed against my chest. Every inch of me responds, needy for her.

Swallowing it down, I focus on the dance and drop to one knee before leaning forward, and she takes her cue easily. Her body dips and she slides her back over mine in a fluid movement as we get lost in the rhythm.

As the crescendo hits, I feel alive again. I haven't had that emotion soar through me in years, and now, for the first time since I walked out and left her crying at the empty bus station as tears streamed down her rosy cheeks, I'm happy. I'm fucking ecstatic and it's all because I'm home.

I'm with Piper.

The song comes crashing to an end, and I realize when silence hits us once more, that I'm holding her in my arms and I'm kissing her. My lips mold to hers. Her tongue tentatively darts out to meet mine.

A soft muffled moan is the only sound she makes because I swallow all her whimpers. I revel in them. I drink them in like they're my sustenance and I know there's no way I can leave her again.

NINETEEN
PIPER

It's silent in the house. Since we danced yesterday, and today, it's been like old times. And now, with Ryder in my old bedroom, it still feels like I'm hiding him away. Although he's been in this house so many times before, this time feels different.

I'm no longer a fifteen-year-old girl who's crushing on her brother's best friend. I'm an adult who has a boyfriend. *Is he my boyfriend?* I don't know. I didn't ask. Perhaps it's too soon to assume so. But I want to. I want to assume everything between Ryder and me is real, that it's not a dream and he's not going to disappear if I blink.

I pull on the sweater, making sure it's warm enough for our plans tonight. Ryder said he wants to take me to the drive-in. Our small town is known for the only working drive-in, so he's proposed a romantic evening watching whatever is playing while we eat hot dogs and drink liters of Coke.

The tingling in my stomach hasn't stopped since I fell asleep on his bed. It's been there, even though just slightly. I don't ignore it, because it's this feeling that's kept me going for four years while he was away.

I head back into my bedroom from the attached bathroom to find Ryder lounging on my armchair. The large ornate one-seater is right at the window, overlooking our vast gardens. I wonder if he knows I used to sit there watching him and Preston play ball in the backyard. Or if he knows I used to sit there only to see how he'd lie out in the sun, tanning his already golden skin while my brother would entertain all the girls he'd brought home.

"You okay there, baby girl?" Ryder questions, setting a magazine he was flipping through on the small table.

"I am. Do I look okay?" I near him, padding closer in my bright purple socks. His hazel eyes track me from head to toe and back again, but he doesn't respond. "What?" I finally ask as he watches me intently.

"Just looking at my beautiful girl."

My cheeks heat with a blush when he rises and closes the distance between us. My arms instinctively wrap around his neck and he leans in to kiss me.

"What is he doing in here?" The deep rumble of my father's livid tone shudders through me like thunder rolling in. A storm is threatening and I know we'll all get caught in it.

"Dad—"

"Don't *Dad* me," he bites out. "Get out of my daughter's bedroom, right now." I've seen my father angry before, but this is ridiculous. We weren't even doing anything.

"Dad, I'm twenty years old," I tell him, hoping he'll calm down, but my father doesn't see anything except the inked bad boy from my youth in my bedroom.

"I'll see you later," Ryder confirms, the sorrow so clear in his deep hazel eyes that they shimmer with guilt. He turns and leaves me with my father.

"No!" I race from the room, only to have my father reach for my bicep, gripping it almost painfully. "Let me go."

"You are my daughter, Piper. Under my roof you live by my rules. This is my house and I will not have you disrespecting me." I tug free from his hold and run down the stairs to find Ryder at the front door.

"Please don't go," I plead, my heart

shattering, fragment by tiny fragment.

"I'll see you soon. He won't listen to me, or you," Ryder tells me what I already know.

My father can be a tyrant. Ryder gently pulls me into a hug. His lips press against the top of my head in a calming kiss, but nothing can keep me from crying. Not right now.

"I want to go with you," I tell him, gripping his T-shirt, holding on to him so tight. I'm scared if I let go, he'll vanish like he did so many years ago.

"Are you still in my house?" My father's venomous growl comes from behind me. His grip on Ryder's shirt tugs him free from me and I'm soon stumbling backward.

"Richard." My mother's voice has me spinning around to see her coming from the kitchen with a cup of tea. "What on earth are you doing?"

"My daughter will not be lumped with a fucking man who cannot offer her anything.

He's already messed up our son's life. Preston was expelled from college because of Ryder Kingsley. Look at him," my father sneers, tugging on Ryder's shirt. "He caused a drunken accident and lost his leg. Do you think I'm going to allow my daughter near the likes of him?"

"I'm an adult. If I want to be with Ryder, I'll be with him."

"Sir, with the utmost respect—"

"Respect?" The laugh my father responds with is livid and angry. He turns to me suddenly, pointing at the staircase. "Get to your room." It's been a while since he spoke to me like a child, like I was disappointing him, but the tone of his voice is enough to have my body vibrating with frustration and anger.

Without responding, I race up the stairs with one quick glance at Ryder. His eyes meet mine and I try to tell him to wait for me with a look. Once in my bedroom, I tug a small hold-all from my closet.

My mind is made up. I need to get out of my father's house. I'll never be happy with the way he wants to rule my life, and that's his fault. Not mine. Stuffing clothes, underwear, and my toothbrush into the bag, I cast a quick glance around, making sure I haven't missed anything vital. Shoving my feet into my sneakers, I make my way back downstairs in time to see Ryder walking out the door.

I sneak past my father. But as soon as I make it out the door, he roars at me. His heated gaze burns into my back. I don't want to look at him, but I can't help turning to face the man I grew up fearing.

"Where the hell are you going?" His voice thunders as he stalks closer to Ryder's car.

"You said I can't be with Ryder while I'm under your roof. Well, I'm making sure I'm no longer under your roof," I tell him, following the man I love as he pulls the passenger door open, allowing me to slide into the seat.

"Get back here, Piper! If you leave you lose everything, and I mean every perk you've become accustomed to." His warning is clear. I'll be cut off from the family money.

"Piper, darling."

I turn to my mother. "I'm sorry, Mom, it's done." I slip into the passenger seat and stare straight ahead. I don't need to see the disappointment in my father's eyes.

"Are you sure about this?" Ryder's gaze is pinned on me. His frown lines crease his forehead and I'm struck by how much I *do* want this. How much I no longer care about the demands of my parents. All my life I've been a pawn in their lives, making sure I was the perfect princess. But I'm not that, nowhere near.

I smile, nod, then whisper. "I've never been surer about anything in my life."

Ryder's smile has always been my

weakness. And right now, he gifts it to me in spades. The grin that makes my heart leap wildly in my chest is plastered on his face, but in his eyes, I see the sadness that it's come to this.

"I'd have to choose at some point, my father would've always given me an ultimatum," I tell Ryder. "And there's no longer a choice in this. You hold my heart. You always will."

My confession has him nodding his head and starting the car. As we make our way down the drive, I know I've made the best decision for me. I'm no longer worried about what other's think. Ryder is mine and I'll always be his.

TWENTY
RYDER

As soon as we reach my apartment, I exit the car and make my way to Piper's door. She's silent, shocked perhaps because when I offer her my hand, she doesn't move.

"Baby girl," I call to her, leaning in so my mouth is at her ear. "I'm here, just let me care for you, please?"

She finally turns to face me, her eyes wide, glistening with tears. "He doesn't love me." Her voice is small, broken and it tugs at my heart. I've wanted her here for so long, but I didn't want it like this.

"I didn't want to come between you and

your family," I tell her as she gets out of the car. Her arms wrap around me, holding on to me like I'm the only thing she needs to breathe. Her face is cocooned in my chest and I can't stop holding her as she finally cries.

Her body shakes as the wetness of her tears soaks through my T-shirt.

"I'm sorry, baby girl," I tell her, pressing my lips to the top of her head.

"It's not your fault, Ryder. Please don't blame yourself," she mumbles into the material, her delicate fingers fisting it, tugging me closer as if she wants to climb inside my clothes.

"I can't not, Butterfly. If I hadn't been there, he would've never gotten angry and cut you off."

She pulls away then to meet my eyes. "He hates everyone who doesn't live up to his standards. There's nothing wrong with you, or us being together. Even Preston is happy for us." She's right. Her father has always had a limited mindset when it came to me, or anyone else who doesn't fit his rigid idea of who his kids should have as friends.

"Let's go inside. We can have something to eat and you can relax." I pull her along, taking the hold-all up to the elevator. The ride up is done in the quiet of just our breaths. I lead her into my apartment again and she settles on the sofa, curling her legs under her ass. She looks so comfortable; like she was always meant to be there. In my space.

Leaving her, I take the small bag into the bedroom, dropping it on the bed. When I enter the living room, she's lying in a ball on the corner of the couch. Her body is so small with her legs curled up, and her arms wrapped around her calves.

"Did you want something to drink? Or eat?"

Her eyes meet mine at my question. "Juice?"

Nodding, I head to the kitchen with my heart heavy that she's walked out of her childhood home because of me. Even though she says it's not my fault, I can't help feel the guilt of what she had to do.

"It's not your fault." Her voice comes from behind me and I realize I've been staring out the window, lost in thought at how to get her back in her father's good graces.

"It is. You might not think so, but you've just practically been disowned because of me. I fuck up everything I touch, and once again, this is no different."

"You always do that," she observes. "You blame yourself for what others do, and that's not fair to you."

Shaking my head, I place the glass of juice on the counter. "Here's your juice." I move past her out of the kitchen and into the living room. Her soft footfalls move behind me and I know she's about to lose her shit with me.

"Do you enjoy it, Ryder?"

Turning to face her, I tip my head to the side. "What, Piper?"

"Taking the blame. It seems you've done it all your life and even now when I need you to believe me, you're convinced it's because of you I've walked out. I would've done it anyway, mainly because I'm an adult," she bites out angrily and I can't help agreeing. Her fire is the first thing I fell in love with, and it's the one thing I've always loved about her. "My father can no longer rule my life. I'm done."

Sitting on the sofa, I pat the cushion beside me, but she shakes her head. I just want her close, to inhale her sweetness. "I get that," I respond. "It's just—"

"No, Ryder, there's no excuse for what he did or said to you, and he doesn't get to tell me who I'm allowed to have in my life." Piper finally nears me, then straddles my lap, her legs on either side of mine. The heat of her on my crotch is making it difficult for me to concentrate on what I wanted to say.

"You don't play fair, Butterfly," I tell her, giving her words back to her. She smiles then, knowing what I mean, then rolls her hips, pressing her core against me. "Jesus, Piper," I grit out, my teeth clenching as I attempt to hold onto my restraint.

"I learned from the best." She smiles down at me. Her fingers trail over my neck, cupping my face as she leans closer, her lips feathering over mine. "I want this, Ryder, I want you."

"Piper, if we do this…"

"We have to," she tells me. "Please." Her plea is enough to have the last thread of control I've been holding onto snap with a loud crack.

"I love when you beg me, baby girl," I growl. My hands find her ass as I grip her and lift her as I rise. Her legs wrap around my hips, her arms around my neck. "Do it again," I command, walking us into the bedroom and setting her on the bed.

"Please, Ryder, I need you."

Reaching for my T-shirt, I pull it up and over my head. "Strip for me." The order is heated, dripping with lust for the woman that's held my heart for most of my life.

She smiles, pulling the hoodie off, giving me a glimpse of her tight tank top. Then, teasingly, she tugs at her top, pulling the material off slowly, and I know she's trying to taunt me. Once it's on the mattress beside her, I take in the pink bra that holds those amazing little tits of hers.

"You're beautiful. Perfect," I tell her. It's true. She's everything I could want or need. And now, I'll finally have her. "Off with those sweatpants."

She pushes the material down her slender legs, showing off the matching panties that hide what I'm dying to see. I watch her scoot up the bed, her legs crossing at the ankle, giving me sneaky glimpses of her material covered pussy.

"Your turn." She smiles, trailing her eyes over my chest, down to the waistband of my pants. Arching an eyebrow, I shove them off, not breaking eye contact with her. Once I'm in only my underwear, I stand there for a moment, giving her one chance to stop me.

"This is it, baby girl," I confirm, leaning against the edge of the bed. My hands grip her legs, tugging her toward me. She moves closer. Her lips are on mine, kissing, licking, and biting at me.

Like the minx she is, her mouth travels to my neck, finding my shoulder. The heat of her breath is enough to have me shooting my load in my boxers.

Moving away from her, I smirk before giving her another order. "I want you out of those panties. Show me what's mine," I tell her.

The corner of her mouth quirks into a grin. I watch the little kitten tug her pink panties down her lithe legs and then I'm met with the glistening pussy that makes my mouth water.

"Fuck."

"What?" she questions, sitting up, attempting to close her legs, but I'm faster. I grip her thighs, pushing them wider.

"You're perfect." Leaning in, I run my nose along her inner thigh, first the left, then the right. Her scent is like honeysuckle, and my tongue darts out to lap at the smooth skin near her pretty pussy.

"Ryder," she moans at my tongue trailing over her and I do it again. "Please, do it." Her pleading is snapping me in two and I can no longer stop. My mouth finds her core, my tongue dipping into her, between her smooth lips, and I drink her in like a fine wine. She's everything I imagined and more.

Her hands fist my hair, tugging and pulling at the strands as I lick and lap at her body. The tremble that travels through her is pure and utter perfection.

"Oh God," she moans loudly, and I wish the whole goddamn city can hear her because this is me claiming the woman I love. Lowering my index finger, I dip it into her, feeling her tighten and pulse around the single digit. She's tight, so fucking tight.

"Are you going to come all over my finger, Butterfly," I coo, allowing my hot breath to fan over her heated core. She's drenched, and I lap at her like a hungry man, starving for more sustenance.

She's sweet, musky, and I feel drunk on her. The best kind of drug I could ever have. The sweetness of my girl. My finger meets resistance and I realize she really did wait for me. I pull away. Gazing up her body, my eyes find hers.

"Ryder, please, please." Her pleas fall toward me, tumbling like raindrops, and I give it to her. I bite down gently on her clit, causing her to whimper and moan, sounds that only make my cock even harder. I smile when I release her hard nub and dart my tongue into her pussy, and she cries out my name over and over again. I don't stop. My mouth continues to devour her until she falls to the mattress spent and mumbling incoherently.

Her essence is all over me. Coating my tongue in the sweetest juices I've ever tasted, and it's all mine.

"Are you ready for me, baby girl?"

She glances up and nods slowly, a small smile on her face. "I've been ready for a long while, Ryder Kingsley. I waited for you, so you better make this worth it." Her sassiness, innocence, and purity shines like a beacon.

"You really did wait," I murmur, still in shock. Most women her age spend their years going out partying, having sex with their high school and college boyfriends, and Piper's right here, still pure. Still a virgin for me.

"I told you, Ryder, there was never anyone else for me." Her words are confident, so sure of herself. "I would've waited forever."

My heart aches at her confession. The fact she knew how she felt and there was no dissuading her to move on.

"Then I better make you never regret your decision." I smile down at her. My hands trail over her legs, reveling in her smooth skin. "Because, once I do this, once I claim you, there's no going back. You're mine."

"I've always been yours."

"I know. And I'll always be yours."

It's a promise. A vow. And I know it's the God's honest truth.

TWENTY ONE

PIPER

Ryder moves away from me for a moment, rising to full height. I watch in awe as he pushes his boxer briefs down. He's naked. Bared to me. In the dim light, his body is a statue carved from colorful marble. His cock, hard and thick, juts from between his hips. His thighs are muscled, tense, and the part of him that's no longer flesh and bone is perfect.

My eyes dart to his, to find him staring at me. "You're everything I ever wanted, Ryder," I tell him. His hands find my thighs, tugging me closer to the edge of the bed. He grips his shaft, slowly stroking it as his gaze bores into me, right through me, right down to my soul.

"And you, my sweet Butterfly, are everything I should have never wanted," he says, placing the tip of his cock against my opening. The metal that's pierced through the underside shines as the light hits it. Sliding it up and down my core, he taunts me, making sure the silver studs glide over my clit, and I wrap my legs around him, tugging him closer.

"Please, just do it, Ryder," I beg. I can't take it anymore. I want to feel him inside me.

He doesn't respond, merely inches into me, and I feel like screaming for more. My body opens around him. The pressure causes me to whimper, but I continue holding on to him. I know if he thinks he's hurting me he'll stop, so I reach for him, holding his one hand while his other guides his cock into me.

The movements are torturous. I can't stop the searing pain that trickles through me when he nudges at the barrier.

"Ryder, fuck me," I grit out through my teeth, frustration and agony dripping on every word. "Just fuck me."

And he does. He pushes into me then, bottoming out inside me, causing my body to shudder and my back to arch from the mattress. I feel full, filled to the brim, and I'm about to explode. He's finally done it. I'm his. Ryder has claimed me and there's no going back now.

His hips rest against my thighs as he lifts my legs on his shoulders. He presses his finger on my clit, circling it slowly, gently, but he doesn't move. He's buried inside me and I'm nothing more than a trembling mess.

"Are you okay?" he questions, his brows furrowed in worry, but I nod. He continues his assault on my hardened nub, making it tingle, and I focus on that. The sensation trickling through me. I'm not sure why he's not moving, but I want him to.

"Yes, I need you to move," I tell him, tears

stinging the corners of my eyes as he slowly pulls out, then dips back into me. He continues the movement, his chest rumbling and his eyes closing as pleasure radiates from him. The pain is stinging, but his fingers taunt and tease me. My own hands tug at the bra I'm wearing and I find my nipples as hard as pebbles.

When I open my eyes, Ryder is staring at me with a hungry look that tells me he likes watching me do this. And I do it to tease him. Tweaking my sensitive nipples, I twist them, making them tighten and peak.

"Fuck, Piper," he growls. "You feel far too good. You're so tight," he hisses tilting his head to the ceiling. His eyes close for a moment as if he's reveling in the feeling as he continues to fuck me. But this isn't fucking. The way he's moving so slowly, his hands massaging my legs, his body connected to mine, this is something far more emotional.

He moves slowly, and my body starts

opening to him even more. The pain is gradually ebbing away along the shore, and I'm left with more want than ever before. There's a gentleness to how the metal inside me, attached to his cock, teases my body, making me tremble with need. I reach down, my hand between my thighs to meet his fingers, and we both tease my clit, making me whimper and moan as pleasure now shoots through me. The movement makes my head spin.

When he finally opens his eyes, he looks between us and smiles. "You're mine, baby girl. I'm going to make you come on my cock," he tells me. I glance down, seeing nothing but the base of his shaft, and I know he's broken me once more, only this time, I wanted it.

He moves faster, leaning in now, allowing my legs to fall from his shoulders, and my feet are perched on the bed. His body cocoons me. His fingers still tease me, still making my body tremble and shake.

"I've always been yours," I confirm, wrapping my arms around his neck.

Ryder lifts me from the bed, walking us over to the wall, pressing my back flush with the cool wooden doorway. "Now, I'm going to make you scream," he promises. His hips roll and I see stars. His cock hits the spot inside me I never knew existed as he continues to drive into me. Faster, harder, with more force than I could imagine.

Our bodies are slick with sweat, but I hold on. My eyes roll back when his mouth finds my neck, his lips suckling on the sensitive flesh, biting down hard, making me yelp.

"I want you to come on my cock, Butterfly," he tells me, his mouth at my ear, his breath hot and his words needy.

He swivels his hips and he once again he hits that one spot. Over and over again. My toes curl as pleasure shoots through me. My head drops back and he takes this opportunity to capture my nipple in his mouth and suck on it through my bra that I realize I didn't remove. The material soaks with his continued suckling and I can't hold back the scream that tumbles from my lips. But I don't call for God, I call for Ryder.

My nails claw at his shoulders and back as my orgasm rockets through me and then I feel him thicken and pulse and I know he's just filled me.

"Fuck."

"Yes."

I'm not sure which one of us says which, but all I can think about is the pleasure that's tingling from my head to my toes. My breathing is fast, my chest rising and falling, and all I want is to do it again.

"Are you okay?" he questions me when I open my eyes, but I nod. I never imagined pleasure so profound, so consuming, but he did everything I needed and I let myself feel.

Yes, the pain was searing, but the pleasure was scorching.

"I've never been more okay," I tell him. Reaching for his face, I hold him steady. "When can we do it again?" I smile, planting a kiss on his lips.

He turns and walks us over to the bed.

"Give me time, woman," he tells me gruffly, causing a laugh to fall from my lips. Setting me on the mattress like I'm made of glass, he slips out of me, causing me to wince at the emptiness I now feel. "Did I hurt you?"

"No, I just don't like not being connected to you."

His eyes burn into mine. His fingers find the heartbeat in my chest and he presses on it gently. "This is where we're connected, always."

"Ryder." My voice is timid, scared. "Promise me this is it." My words cause him to frown. "I mean... you're not leaving again.

Right?"

"I'm never leaving again." He smiles, giving me another kiss before leaving me on the bed and making his way into the bathroom. When he returns, he's carrying a soft wet cloth, which he uses to gently towel between my thighs. Once we're both settled in bed, he pulls me closer, holding me like his life depends on it, and for a brief second, I wonder if it does.

TWENTY TWO
RYDER

I'm sitting in the classroom three days after feeling Piper's body pulse around me and it's the only thing I can think of. When we finally took the final step in our relationship I knew what I need to do. Later today, I'll head out with Preston and buy a ring. As much as I want to ask her father's permission to propose, I know he'll refuse me at every turn, so the next best person to go to would be my best friend.

Piper's still young, and I'm not going to steal her away from her family, but I want to claim her forever. I love her, and pushing her away for so long was my mistake. I've lost years I'll never get back, but she's accepted me at my worst, and I know she'll love me forever.

Her eyes meet mine across the room, and I offer her a smile. She's so good with those kids, and I can't help wondering if we'll ever have a few of our own. One or two. Perhaps more.

She'd look so beautiful pregnant, swollen, and glowing while she's carrying our children.

"You okay there, Mr. Kingsley?" Her gentle voice snags me from the visions in my mind.

"I am," I tell her, rising to full height, pulling her closer. "I was just thinking I'd love to take you home for dinner."

"We can order in," she tells me innocently.

"I wasn't talking about food," I whisper in her ear, making her shiver in anticipation of what's to come.

"Behave yourself," Piper admonishes me, swatting my arm and leaving me at the stereo to curate the music. She smiles at the students, all of them looking up at her like she's an angel. She is. The way she moves about the room, light on her feet, fluid in the way her body dips and rolls, showing the kids how to count the beats, to hop onto their hands from a low stance is mesmerizing.

My phone vibrating drags my attention away from the beautiful woman to a message that stops my heart. I didn't think I could run away from my past, I didn't even think I could forget what I'd done, but it seems it's caught up with me and when I glance up at Piper once more, I know I have to leave before she finishes her routine. I can't explain what's going on, but I need to fix this before the shit gets near my perfect girl.

"You did what?" Preston's voice is livid, rage drenching every word he spits down the line at me. I didn't have a choice. He knows it as well as I do.

"Dude, you know your father had a hand

in this. He hates me," I tell him. I'm met with silence. He does know the truth. Nobody else would've had me packing my bags and heading back to Los Angeles faster than Mr. Beaufort himself.

"I'll figure it out," he informs me. "In the meantime, just message Piper and tell her you haven't in fact fucked off and broken her heart again."

"I will, as soon as I get back to our apartment." I hang up before he can give me another earful and take the turn off to the building we'd been living in while we were in LA. The large three-bedroom place had been our home for four years, and when we left, one of the guys we'd lived with offered to take it off our hands with the agreement that if we're ever back in town, we'd have a place to crash.

My phone buzzes again, and I know it's Piper. I don't have to look at the screen to see her name glaring at me, accusing me of doing what I promised not to do. I've fucked it up again, and this time, I doubt she'll ever forgive me.

Once I pull into a parking spot, I exit the car and make my way to the elevator. The second floor apartment was the easiest access for me, and the guys both decided they'd be happy to share it with me when we moved out here.

When I reach the door, I unlock it and shove it open. The living room greets me when I step inside, along with silence, informing me that Logan isn't here. Shutting the door, I shrug off my hoodie and grab my phone from my pocket. Like I thought, Piper's name is burning a hole through the screen.

Sighing, I hit call and press the device to my ear. On the second ring she answers.

"Where are you? Are you okay? Preston said you had to leave," she tells me breathlessly, and I picture her running around my apartment looking for me. Her breathing is harsh over the line and I'm certain she's panicked.

"I needed to do something out here, sign some documents." The lie feels like poison on my tongue, but I can't tell her why I'm really here. If she knows, she'll never forgive her father. As much as I dislike him, I want her to have a relationship with him one day. If I can just get the charge brought against me dropped without worrying her, then we'll be fine.

"Why didn't you tell me?" she questions, hurt evident in her voice, and it cracks my heart in two. "I could've come with you."

"No, it's something I need to do alone, Piper. Please, just let me do this. Can you wait for me?" This time, I'm the one begging. I'm pleading with her to give me time, to wait for me like she waited before. And she did. She fucking waited four years for me to return and claim her like she was always meant to be mine. I don't know how long this will take, or how much she'll be able to offer me, but I wait for her response, my heart thudding violently in my chest, making my ribs ache.

There's a heart-wrenching agony in loving someone and leaving them. It can sting, it can hurt, but it's when you lose that someone, when they can no longer give you another chance, that's when it kills you.

The same way the words from my doctor's mouth broke my heart and mind when he told me I'd never have both my legs again, this torment of not knowing how to fix what I did is haunting me. And Piper's father knows it.

"Ryder, you know I'll wait forever for you," she finally tells me. "I just need you to do something for me."

"Anything—"

"Don't tell me you'll do one thing and then act out another. Don't promise not to break my heart and then shatter it all over the goddamn floor."

Her anger is warranted. I messed up. I did

promise her I'd never leave, but this time I had no choice. It was forced on me.

"The next time I look into your eyes, I'll make a promise, Piper, and it will be for life."

I hang up, leaving her to ponder on my words while I walk into the small office we set up while I was recovering. All the documents that were signed are in there, and I know if I'm going to clear my name, I'll find what I need in here.

TWENTY THREE

PIPER

Frustration is something I've lived with all my life. From having parents who never understood me, to a brother who acted like he hated me. And now, I'm in love with a man who'd rather be away from me than to tell me what the hell is going on.

"Piper." The deep voice of my father startles me. Spinning around, I find him standing in the doorway to the classroom. His large frame looms in the small space, making him look even scarier than he already is.

"What are you doing here?" I question. I haven't seen him since he told me never to come back. I chose Ryder, and my father was livid, but to see him here makes me wonder what his game plan is.

My father is one of those men who always has something up his sleeve. As a lawyer, he has to. It's part of his job. But I'm not his job, I'm his daughter, and I wish he'd treat me like that.

"I've missed you, Piper," he tells me, strolling into the space. "Also, I need to show you something." He hands me a folder I didn't notice him holding when he first entered.

"What is this?" Taking it, I flip it open to find what looks like a police report. Ryder's name front and center as the person who was driving the night of the accident he told me about.

"Your boyfriend," my father spits the word at me. "He's responsible for almost killing your brother."

I open my mouth to speak, but words

evade me at that moment. Anger turning my blood red-hot, but it's a voice behind him that stills me.

"No, he's not."

We both turn to face the doorway where Preston is standing. He glances between us, then saunters closer. My heart aches at that moment when I realize my brother had something to do with Ryder's accident.

"Ryder wasn't drunk that night." His words sound like an echo, and I shake my head to clear it. "He had two beers all night, nothing else. He wasn't drunk," Preston says, dropping his gaze to the floor. "I was the one who was smashed. He took the car keys from me when I told him I wanted to drive the two girls home."

"This is ridiculous," my father hisses. "You both want to protect a delinquent of a boy."

My brother raises his head, meeting my father's angry glare dead-on. "You think he's a delinquent?" The chuckle that rumbles in

Preston's chest is incredulous. "Have you looked at your own son, old man?" He steps forward and my body is rigid. Fear trickles through me and I'm certain there's going to be a fight.

"Preston, just let him think what he—"

"No, Piper, it's time dear old Dad hears me, listens to the truth he's been ignoring for so long." My brother glances my way. With a nod, he turns his attention back to our father, who is positively vibrating with rage. "I'm the one who got in the driver's seat and forced my best friend to practically knock me out to get me to sit in the back. I was the one who let him get in the car and drive that night."

The sadness and guilt that drips from my brother's words make my chest hurt. My heart slams into my ribs, and I have to swallow back the anger and fury that threatens to pull me under.

"I'm the one who caused the accident,

because I was playing a stupid game of chance by blocking his eyes, chuckling that he couldn't see where he was going." The confession hangs in the air surrounding us, heavy, drenched in the guilt of my brother and the rage of my father.

I want to slap my brother. I want to punch him, hit him, I want to scream and shout at him, but I don't, because when I look up at him again, I tell him with one glare how much I hate him.

His expression is filled with sorrow, but I don't care. I no longer want him in my life. He is responsible for Ryder being as broken as he is, and I don't mean physically, I mean mentally and emotionally.

"Get out, Dad. I need you to get out and never come near me or Ryder again. Preston, I need time to figure this out. I don't know how to feel right now other than angry and confused."

"Piper—"

"No, Father," I bite out in frustration. "I'm done with this anger you hold toward Ryder for nothing. He's a good man. He has a good head on his shoulders. He's got plans for the future and all you can see is the fact he has tattoos and piercings. I'm done with this. I need you both to leave."

A grunt from my father is all I get, but I know what it means. He'll be back and even though I've told him I don't want him near me again, he'll do something stupid to win me back, only this time, there is no winning me back.

My brother steps forward, but I hold out a hand to stop him. "Just go. I'll call you later." He nods, presses a hand on mine, and turns to leave me in the classroom.

TWENTY FOUR

RYDER

A knock on the door of the apartment drags me from the paperwork in front of me. The girls Preston and I had in the car that night were sisters. Their father decided to drag what happened in the past back into our lives by suing me, only I know it's because Mr. Beaufort spoke to him. As a lawyer, he must've been able to dredge up some fancy terms and conditions to make the man do this.

We've paid. I may have paid more than the others, but that doesn't matter. I was the one driving that night. It doesn't matter what happened with Preston. It was my hands on wheel.

Another knock tells me that whoever it is won't go away and I wonder if Preston decided to drive out here. Rising from my seat, I make my way to the front door. When I pull it open, it's not my best friend, but his sister on the other side.

"What are you doing here, Piper?"

"I need to see you, and I need you to listen to me," she tells me, lifting her chin in defiance, and I can't help but step back and allow her into the apartment.

Shutting the door, I turn to watch her settle herself on the sofa. When I join her, she turns to me, meeting my gaze.

"Preston confessed what happened that night," she tells me in a whisper, her fingers twirling the material of her hoodie. "Why didn't you tell me, Ryder?"

She's right, I should've, but I'd become accustomed to telling my story, not Preston's, that it was just something I said. It's how I told everyone what happened.

"Ryder, look," she says, placing a hand on my thigh, her thumb circling the part of me that's no longer flesh and bone, but plastic and metal. And as much as it should be a strange sensation not to feel her touch, it's not, because it doesn't matter where Piper is, or what she's doing, I'll always feel her. She'll always be a part of me.

"I didn't tell you because I didn't want you to hate Preston." I turn my gaze to the window, looking at the cloudless blue sky and it reminds me of my girl's eyes on a summer day.

"I don't hate Preston anymore. Growing up I did, he was never nice to me. He wasn't the brother that would look after me. But right now, with everything that's happened, I'm just livid that he allowed you to take the blame for it, and I'm angry at you for not telling me sooner. If we do this, Ryder, I need honesty."

Her words catch my attention. There's an honesty in her eyes that grips my chest painfully. *She still wants me?* Shaking my head, I sigh, knowing she is right, but I don't understand how she can still want me after everything that's happened.

"I didn't tell you because I knew you'd hate your brother. He's your family, Piper, blood, and I'm nobody to you."

"That's bullshit, Ryder," she bites out angrily. Then suddenly, she's on my lap, straddling me like she always does. "Look at me, look into my eyes and tell me you're nobody to me," she commands. Her delicate hands on my face hold me steady so I can't turn away.

"I can't. You know I can't tell you that because you know I love you, and I know you love me," I tell her, holding on to her hips, my fingers digging into the smooth, silky flesh I know is hidden under her clothes.

"So, don't you dare tell me we're nothing to each other," she insists. "I'm angry, Ryder, so goddamn angry at Preston." This time, she curls herself in my lap, her arms wrapping around me as she nuzzles her head under my chin. The scent of honeysuckle from her hair has me inhaling deeply.

"Your father—"

"I know what he did, that's why I'm here," she mumbles into my shirt. "But I don't want to talk about him right now." Her words are muffled by the material of my T-shirt, but I hear her. "I want to talk about you and me."

I pull in a breath, holding it before I question her, "What about you and me?"

"You said something on the phone last night. You told me that the next promise you make me would be forever," she reminds me of the words I'd uttered. "What did you mean?"

Her big blue eyes shine with as much curiosity as a kitten when it first gets a toy. I allow my gaze to memorize every inch of her face, from the gold strands of her hair that fall over her cheeks to the button nose that crinkles each time she gets frustrated at me, down to those plump rosy lips that make me groan with want.

"I meant, Piper... I meant I love you. I always have." My voice is raspy when I look into her eyes. "It's no secret. I never knew I could care about someone so much. I wanted what was best for you and I didn't care about what happened to me."

My throat feels like there's a lead weight stuck in it.

"When I got hurt, all I wanted was to walk away from you because I knew you deserved more, you deserved better." She opens her mouth to speak, but I place a finger on her lips to keep her quiet. "I wanted to walk away because it would've been best, in my mind. But, I realize it's not best because we complete each other, Piper. And what I meant when I said that last night is that I want you. Forever."

This isn't how I wanted to propose.

It's not romantic.

I don't have a ring.

All I have are my words.

"Are you asking me to marry you, Ryder Kingsley?"

TWENTY FIVE
PIPER

He smiles. *That smile.* The ring in his lip glistens in the light that's streaming through the window. It hits the metal just right, making the ring look like a gem. Shiny and new.

"Perhaps," he responds with his eyes twinkling mischievously. "I wanted to make it more romantic, you know, ask Preston's permission and all that shit." His words make me laugh, the sound trickling through the space, and I can't help leaning in closer to him.

"You don't need to ask anyone's permission, Ryder. You just need me to say yes," I tell him, planting a kiss on his neck, suckling the skin into my mouth, causing a growl to rumble in his chest.

"Baby girl," he warns. "If you keep that up, I'll have to carry you to the bedroom."

"Mmmm, and what will happen if you carry me into the bedroom?" I question, moving my lips higher, finding the piercing in his ear, gently tugging it with my teeth.

"Fuck," Ryder grunts when I roll my hips while trailing my tongue over the shell of his ear. "I'm going to fuck you, Butterfly." It's another warning. One that makes me tingle between my legs, and I can't help a soft whimper that tumbles free from my lips.

"Then you better show me, Ryder."

Swiftly, he lifts me up as he rises from the sofa and we're heading down a long hallway toward a door that's slightly ajar. Entering the space is like walking into Ryder's bedroom back home. With jet color curtains and a black carpet, along with charcoal bed sheets, it's indeed filled with darkness, but it makes me feel safe.

"Stay," he tells me, setting me on the edge of the mattress, leaving me in his bedroom. I hear him stroll back down the hall, then the sound of glasses, or at least, I think it's glasses, makes its way toward me. When Ryder returns, he's carrying a glass, a can of soda, and some ice.

"What is that for?" I question, watching him set the items on the nightstand. He doesn't respond, merely opens the can and takes a long swig.

"Now, little lady." The corner of his mouth kicks up into a sinful smirk. "It's time for me to devour you." The look on his face is positively ravenous. "I want you to take that pretty top off for me," his husky voice orders, and my fingers have a mind of their own, obeying him. Once I'm in my bra, his gaze darkens.

"Anything else you'd like me to get rid of, Mr. Kingsley?" I tease playfully.

"All of it, baby girl. I want you on my bed, naked, spread open so I can look at how beautiful you are without anything hindering my view." Ryder steps back, watching me intently as I toe off my sneakers, then slowly pushing the jeans I'm wearing to the floor. My bright pink socks hit the carpet, and then it's just me in my white panties and matching bra.

"You know," I tell him, rising from the mattress, "I think it's unfair that I have to get undressed, and you're standing there in your T-shirt and sweatpants."

Another wolfish smile tilts his lips. He reaches for the material of his shirt and tugs it from his tall, lean frame. His chest, down to his torso is toned, chiseled with dips and peaks I'm dying to tease with my tongue.

There's a dark trail of hair below his belly button that dips below the waistband of his underwear. Ink adorns him. Beautiful intricate patterns of black and color, all over his smooth, tanned flesh. When I meet his hungry gaze, I offer a sultry smile. I've never flirted before, never been in front of a boy, correct that, a man, in my underwear. But the way Ryder looks at me makes everything south of my belly button tingle.

He silently discards his pants and soon we're leveled on the playing field. Him in tight black briefs, and me in white. A contrast. But together, we match perfectly.

Reaching back, I unclasp my bra and allow it to fall at my feet. Ryder's heated stare trails over me, down to my chest, then he meets my gaze.

"You're far too perfect for me." His words are warm, affectionate, and I want to refute him, but he shakes his head. "But, I've come to the conclusion that perfection is all mine." He steps forward, gripping my hips, pulling me closer. "And I'll never let it go again."

He leans in. His lips find mine, warm and

demanding, and I allow him control of the kiss. His tongue gently snakes into my mouth, tasting, licking, as if he's savoring me with every movement.

His fingers dig into my hips, eliciting a whimper from me, which he swallows in the kiss. My arms wrap around his neck, pulling him closer. His hands find my ass, lifting me against him as he turns to sit on the mattress.

"I want to fuck you," he tells me, "but I have a better idea."

"Oh?"

He nods, shuffling up the bed and leaning against the headboard. I'm still straddling his lap when he reaches between us with one hand, shoving my panties to the side. His fingers find my entrance.

"You're so wet, Butterfly," he groans as he circles my clit, his index finger dipping into me, teasing me as he finger fucks me. It slides into me so easily and glides back out, over and over again. My hips roll against him, making him harder beneath me.

"Please, Ryder." My plea is unanswered as he continues his ministrations on my body. The glint in his eye is pure devilish as he taunts me, his thumb pressing my clit, teasing the hardened nub, and then he pulls his fingers from my core and his cock is there, ready, hard, and he gently slides into me.

It takes a moment for me to acclimate to his thickness, the metal of his piercing rubbing against my inner walls, making my toes curl as pleasure rockets through me. I've never been so turned on, so needy. Ryder's mouth finds my nipple, suckling the bud, grazing it with his teeth.

It feels as if my body is electrified, every nerve sparking, every synapse firing, and I'm crying out as he continues to drive into me. Faster, harder. His body rigid, mine purely putty in his hands.

"That's my baby girl," he coos, his voice drenched with desire, my body his instrument as he plays me like a maestro in an orchestra. There are no fast beats, only gentle, loving melodies, and I cry out as his fingers tweak my clit, his cock hitting that spot inside me, and I see stars burst behind my eyelids.

"Ryder."

"So fucking perfect."

TWENTY SIX
RYDER

The cell is cold. Thankfully, I'm alone, but that's not what worries me. I'm more concerned about my girl. I know Piper is probably going out of her mind right now. I don't know what's happening, or why they've arrested me this morning, but I'm certain it's got something to do with her father.

Lying back, I rest my arm across my eyes, blocking out any light that's left streaming through the bars of my small cell. I can't think of Piper coming back to the apartment after going to grab some coffee to find me gone. I can't imagine what she's probably feeling right now. I gave her a small promise ring, and then they dragged me off.

I shut my eyes and recall the day I woke up with a missing limb. The day I thought my life had ended. I'd never been more scared, angrier, and more anguished.

"Mr. Kingsley." The man in the white coat and blue shirt smiles down at me. A doctor. My mind replays the events that led me here. Stupidity and recklessness.

"Yes," I croak out a response.

The man smiles more. "You were all very lucky," he tells me, but the needle that's been stuck in my arm pumps liquid into me and I know it's some form of painkillers.

"Where is Preston?"

"Mr. Beaufort and the two ladies are fine. They're being kept for observation but should be released soon. Mr. Kingsley, there's something I needed to talk to you about." His expression

changes from smiling to serious and my chest aches with fear.

"Something's happened?" I question, my voice cracking and my throat burning.

"We tried everything we could, but your leg, Mr. Kingsley, unfortunately we had to—"

"What?!" My voice booms around me, making me wince in agony. My eyes snap toward the bed and I see it, where both my legs should be, there's only one under the sheet. My right leg, or what's left of it, is hidden by the clinical white covers, but it ends halfway down.

Tears sting my eyes. Even though I'm highly medicated, and I can't feel the pain, it's a phantom agony that sets in and the monitors on my chest are beeping wildly.

"I need you to calm down, Mr. K—"

"Calm down? Calm the fuck down?" I roar, attempting to pull the drip from my arm, and the door flies open as two bulky men enter and hold me down. "Let me go. Don't fucking touch me!"

The doctor pulls out a needle and proceeds pushing it into the connector where the drip is slowly administering my pain meds and as soon as the syringe is empty, I feel tired.

My eyes flit open and closed. And the last thing I see when my eyes shut, is Piper's pretty blue eyes, long golden hair, and her sweet smile.

Opening my eyes, I push off the bed and head toward the bars. The place is busy, noisy, but my mind is awash with memories of my girl. Images of her keep me sane. I can't call for anyone. There's nobody here to help me. I'm about to lie down again when a man in a tailored suit saunters up to my cell.

"Mr. Kingsley," the well-dressed man says. "Your father posted bail. You'll be out of here in a few moments. We're handling the case Mr. Beaufort has created against you."

"I don't understand. What case?" My question causes him to sigh, and I wonder if this is some sick joke Piper's father is playing at.

The man stares at me for a moment before responding. "He's laid a claim that you kidnapped his daughter. We found her at your apartment about an hour ago, and she's verified her father's false accusation. That's the reason you've been let out on bail."

"I know he's angry because she chose to live with me and move out of his house, but this is ridiculous," I tell him angrily. Frustration grips me in its feral claws that this asshole is even attempting to start this shit. When the police officers arrived early this morning, Piper had left to buy coffee down the road. I'd found her note telling me she'd be right back. I can't imagine the panic she must've felt returning to find me gone.

The man nods at my explanation. "We had all that verified when Ms. Beaufort came forward this morning. The problem is, he's now requesting a restraining order against you."

"And can he get away with this? I haven't hurt anyone. His daughter is safe with me, you saw her. She chose to be with me rather than go home with him."

He nods in agreement. "That's why your father has contested it. You'll be home in a few hours and the order will be dropped. Don't worry. Your father has faith in you." His words still me for a moment. Even though we had a heart to heart, I feel like my father having an ounce of faith in me is a gift in itself. Something I'd never had before.

"Thank you."

I'm left alone again, and I have a moment to collect my thoughts on Mr. Beaufort and his fucking anger toward me. It doesn't make sense. How is it that out of all Preston's friends, I'm the one he hates so much? I've never done anything to him or his family, so it doesn't make any sense.

"Ryder." My girl's voice is like an angel song when she appears outside the cell. "Oh my God, you're okay," she whimpers, anguished.

"What are you doing here, Piper?"

"I needed to see if you're okay. My father has lost his mind," she tells me. "I don't know what he's trying to do, but this isn't going to make me run home and tell him I love him. I cannot believe he put you in here."

I can tell she's livid. Her voice heightens with every word and her body is positively vibrating with anger.

"I'll be out in a few hours. My father's lawyer said they've contested the allegations. I'll be okay, baby girl. I don't want you in a place like this."

"I don't want *you* in a place like this."

I know when Piper is adamant about something, nothing can sway her decision, and this is no different. She's going to fight me tooth and nail if I ask her to leave, so I don't. Instead, I enjoy the time she's with me, even though this place is a shithole.

It only took an hour and I was released. I'm not sure what I would've done if my father hadn't stepped in. I'm far too proud to call him, and I know Piper would've had no sway with her dad. The man hates me. It's no secret.

We came straight to the apartment. The first thing I needed was a shower. There's nothing that could ever compare to being locked inside a jail cell. The night of the accident, I'd only had two beers, so when they tested my blood alcohol limit I was under the legal allowance, so there wasn't any question as to who had actually been more intoxicated. The car we hit had two teenagers who'd been drinking so much they were close to alcohol poisoning by the time they'd smacked into us.

Even though it wasn't wholly their fault, I

knew that if they'd been sober, they would've seen us, or even been able to swerve out of the way. And this is why I no longer drink. Alcohol, drugs, anything that can change your mindset and inhibitions is not something I need in my life.

Even though Preston and Jeremiah have the odd beer, they're both done with their younger partying days, which I'm thankful for. I sound so much older than I am. Almost twenty-four and I could pass as a middle-aged man.

"I can't walk, Preston," I bite out angrily. I'm angry. I fucking hate the world and having him right beside me after what he did doesn't help my mood. I can't forgive him. Not right now. Maybe not ever. Even though we both played a part in what happened, I'm the one who lost everything.

"Look, I know you hate me. I fucking hate me," *he continues. There's no need for him to tell me this. We both know my life is over. I'll never be able to*

dance again. I'll never be able to go to Piper and tell her all the things I want to give her because I can't.

Yes, there's the option of a prosthetic. I will probably be able to walk again, but my love, the one thing that gave me solace—besides the girl I love— is gone. The dream I came out here for is no longer within my grasp.

I glance down at the missing part of me. Where my foot should've been, is nothing. Half a fucking man. Anger surges through me along with pain. Agonizing fucking pain.

"Preston, get out of my face."

"Maybe if Piper—"

"I said get the fuck away from me. Don't you think you've done enough?" Our eyes meet in a standoff, rage from me, guilt from him. Good, he should feel guilty. He should hate himself as much I hate me. Shaking my head, I wheel the chair away from him and into the bedroom, slamming the door shut behind me.

Done.

All fucking done.

"Ryder." Piper's voice drags me from the errant thoughts. She steps into my bedroom wearing a T-shirt that just about hangs below her ass. "I made you some coffee," she says innocently, then sets it down, and I notice she's wearing a tiny pair of panties with a pink lace trim that makes me harder than a steel pole.

"What the fuck are you wearing?"

She spins on her bare foot, her big blue eyes meeting mine. "Your T-shirt." She shrugs nonchalantly. "Why?"

"Did you just go out there, where Logan is, dressed like that?" Rage and jealousy rear their ugly heads as I watch her watch me.

She smiles. "I like when you're all jealous and growly." Her delicate hand waves my way as if it's a fucking joke.

"Piper—"

"Calm yourself. Logan left about an hour

ago. He said he had work to do. He's weird, you know."

"Yeah, I know. But I don't want you walking out there like this." I stalk closer to her, taking her hands and tugging her closer to me. "And I growl because you're mine."

"I think it's hot." She smiles, trailing her fingers over my bare chest. "Oh, your lawyer called and said everything's been sorted out. My dad, however, has been calling me nonstop. He's left a voice message to tell me he wants to talk to me tomorrow night."

"You should go," I tell her. "He *is* your father after all, and since my dad has given me an olive branch, perhaps yours will realize I'm not going anywhere. I've learned forgiveness is easier to live with than anger."

"When did you get so philosophical?"

"When I almost died and lost you forever." My honesty makes her brows crease and her nose wrinkle.

"I don't like you talking like that. Tell me something nice."

"I love you, Piper Beaufort. I'll always love you."

"I guess that will do." She laughs. "And I love you, Ryder Kingsley, and I can't wait to be your wife."

"And have the twelve kids I want?" I chuckle, pulling her even closer.

"Twelve?" Her mouth falls open in shock. "No way, mister. Two, max."

Leaning in, I place a kiss on her pouty lips. "One day, I'll revel in seeing your body change, and I can't wait to see you pregnant with my baby. But we'll be responsible and wait. I want to give you everything, Piper. A career, a family, and I want to make every dream you have come true."

"You've already given me the one I've wanted since the moment you smiled at me," she informs me with another kiss on the lips.

"You."

"Good, there's nothing else I'll ever want."

"Ryder," she says, as if she's about to ask something I'd rather not tell her. But she's with me for life, so anything Piper wants to know, I'll confess. "Did you ever really hate my brother for the accident?"

"There was a time, a very long while where I didn't talk to Preston. I pushed everyone away. I guess, deep down, I never wanted to admit I needed people in my life." Sighing, I reach for her face, cupping the smooth skin beneath my hand. I allow the pad of my thumb to gently stroke a circle on her cheek.

"You do need people in your life. Me, Preston, even though he can be an asshole, and Jeremiah, we all love you. And your dad. He was there when you needed him."

"I know. At the time I didn't see it that way. I'd lost a part of myself, physically, but I also lost my dream. We were young men doing stupid things. I'm not sure if the accident would've happened if Pres didn't do what he did, but I look at it this way—I spent three years angry. Fuck, if I'm truly honest, I spent my life angry at someone, whether it was my dad, my mom, and myself."

"How did you forgive him?"

"About six months before we came home, he did something stupid. There was a girl he'd been seeing. She was bad news, but your brother wanted her. Jer and I tried to warn him off, but Preston is a stubborn asshole."

"That he is," she agrees with a smile.

"This girl got herself into trouble with some drug dealer in LA. She was off her head one night and Preston went to confront the fucker. Needless to say, your brother was in the hospital for a few weeks. But..." I recall the moment I knew that forgiving him would be easier on myself than holding onto anger. "When I saw him lying there in that hospital bed, I knew that if something had happened to him, I'd be lost. He was there for me when I almost died, twice in my life. And I needed him."

"I'm glad you're still friends." She plants a kiss on my cheek and holds on to me. Her slender arms wrap around my neck as she nuzzles into my neck. Closing my eyes, I let myself enjoy her warmth, her sunshine.

TWENTY SEVEN
PIPER

This morning when I woke up, I'd had five missed calls from my mother. My father insisted in a voicemail, that I come talk to them. *To sort things out*, he said. Something in his tone told me there was more drama coming my way. I know he doesn't approve of Ryder, and that's not my problem anymore, that's my father's own judgment. He doesn't have to like Ryder. He doesn't even have to tolerate him, because I've made my choice, and I won't waver.

The house is formidable from the outside. The open brick allows you to see the beauty, the outer appearance that my family has always been about. Nothing on the inside matches how beautiful it is on the outside. *Just like my family*, I think.

Pushing open the heavy front door, I make my way inside, the click resounding loudly in my ears as a warning. I'm inside the Beaufort mansion and I feel less at home than I am when I'm in Ryder's small apartment. When I step into the living room, I find my parents sitting side by side. My mother's hands are twisted around each other and I know she's nervous. Her face tells me everything.

"You wanted to see me," I say before seating myself opposite them. This was my father's idea, but it will be the last time he ever sees me. After what happened with Ryder, I no longer want anything to do with him or his rules.

"Piper, what I did—"

"Was wrong, unforgivable," I tell him. "Father, you cannot use your influence to rule everyone else's life. You've lost me, and you've lost Preston. Don't you see what you're doing?" Tears sting my eyes when I look at him, seeing how he's hardened over the years. I know that parents are meant to keep their children safe, but he's become a tyrant and I'm no longer allowing him to control me like a robot.

"I'm your father and that poor excuse of a boy is not good for you." His insistence about Ryder is frustrating. He just doesn't see what's right in front of him. "You and your brother will soon see that he'll bring you down."

"Why? What has he ever done to you to make you hate him so much?" I question, my voice rising with every word.

"It isn't your business to know what your parents choose for you," he spits out, his face turning bright red, and I wonder if the vein in his forehead will pop.

"What you choose for me?" I let out a humorless laugh and rise. "This meeting is over. It will be the last one you ever get."

"Piper, please," my mother finally opens her mouth. After years of letting daddy dearest run the house, run our lives, I turn to her, waiting for her to finally say something I want to hear. "I made a mistake a long time ago."

My heart kicks in my chest at her words. I inhale a sharp breath, waiting, my fingers tingling with anxiety at what she's about to tell me. *Please don't say what I think you're going to say, Mother*. Don't you dare. Don't. Please. No. No. No.

"I had... I had... an affair," she finally stumbles over her confession.

"What? Are you trying to tell me...?" My words fall into nothing, silence, heavy and laden with confusion. Fearful that she's about to tell me something bad, something that's about to knock my world on its axis.

"Preston is your half-brother," she mumbles. "He and Ryder share a father."

My mouth falls open, but the words I want to voice don't come out. My body is trembling with the news that I'm only Preston's half-sister only. But more than that, relief settles in my stomach that Ryder is not related to me in any way.

"You cheated on Dad?" I rasp, confusion setting itself heavily in my gut at the thought of my parents being other than the utterly in love couple they portray.

"I did. I made a mistake and I pay for it every day, Piper," she whispers, shame so clear on her face. "I was young and impressionable."

"That's what those Kingsley men prey on," my father hisses through clenched teeth.

Shaking my head, I step closer to them both, to my mother who's now crying when I glance her way. "No. This is ridiculous that you can put Mr. Kingsley's wrongdoing on Ryder. He's not the bad guy here." I point at my mother then, feeling every bit as angry as my father looks. "This is on you," I tell her. "Both of you, don't come near me or Ryder, or even Preston again."

Spinning on my heel, I make for the doorway, but my father's strong hand grips my arm, tugging me around.

"Listen to me, and listen good," he rumbles. "If you walk out that door, there's no coming back in here. I forgave your mother years ago for what she did, but I will not have my daughter messing up her life because of a Kingsley."

My heart cracks. My chest aches, but my mind is set. I've seen my father angry so many times before. His temper has always been something that we as kids have been wary of, but this is beyond any of that, and I no longer care.

"Then I'll never ever see you again." My response causes a whimper from my mother, and it turns my father's face purple with rage.

"This isn't on Preston or me. We no longer have to answer to your tyrannical ways. Now, let go of my arm because you're hurting me."

Tugging away from him, I turn and make my way to the door once again. My mother's emotional pleading echoes behind me, but I don't care. When I reach the car, I slip into the driver's seat and sigh, realizing what I've just done.

It all comes crashing down around me and I can't stop the tears.

Anger, frustration, happiness, and sadness all rush through me like a melody kicking back loudly as it vibrates through me.

My family is torn apart because of lies and secrets.

Starting the engine, I blink away the salty drops of emotion and take a cleansing breath before making my way back to the apartment.

To my home.

To Ryder.

TWENTY EIGHT

RYDER

My brother. Well, half-brother. This shit is weird. Like those damn soap operas that my mother used to get hooked to. I'm still trying to wrap my head around it when Piper strolls into the living room.

"Preston is coming for dinner," she informs me, settling her pert little ass on my lap. "He's still trying to come to terms with the news as well."

"For years I believed that my father was an asshole, and this just proves he was. But, it doesn't make sense. Why your mother? I mean, our folks never saw eye to eye." Shaking my head, I reach for Piper, pulling her closer to my chest. "I've always wanted a brother, and Preston was pretty much it for so long that finding out we are related is great. I think I'm just disappointed in my father. You know?"

"I do. My mother always used to harp on about me being perfect, making sure I had all the right clothes, said all the right things, but she was the one who'd messed up."

"Are you ready for the showcase tomorrow?" I ask her, changing the subject before the past takes away from the fact she's got her first showcase as a teacher tomorrow.

She nods. "The kids are. I don't know if I am."

"What do you mean? You've done an amazing job with them." And she has. I haven't been there for all the classes, but I know Piper would've made sure they were all ready for their big debut.

"I just wanted to be there on stage with

them, just once, you know?"

"Then do it." I urge her. "I love you, baby girl, and you should be up there."

She looks at me with affection and happiness in those big blue eyes. My lips find hers, and I can't stop tugging her even closer. Each time we're together feels like it's new, exciting, and I know I love her with all my heart. I want her to go up there and dance, to enjoy the freedom that music offers us.

"I wish you were up there with me," she mumbles against my mouth.

I should be beside her, but I can't. There's no way I can bring myself to step onto a stage, not with my leg. It's taken years for me to build the courage to teach dance, to even get up and dance for myself. Having people watch me is not something I want to do.

The doorbell sounds down the hallway and Piper is up and heading that way. I follow behind, knowing I'm about to see Preston again.

Since the confession, he's been scarce and now I get to meet my half-brother, officially.

"Hey, Pip," I hear him greet his sister. I enter the living room and meet his gaze as he turns my way. "Bro." He smirks. "Didn't think it would be as official as it is now, but since we're related, sort of."

"I think we've always been brothers, just not by blood," I tell him, pulling him into a hug. "Piper made dinner." I gesture to the table in the dining room. It's set for three, and I know my girl went all out. This apartment will soon be history when Piper and I move to LA, and I'll miss this space.

"Thanks, Pip." He pulls her into his arms and presses a kiss to the top of her head. "I always knew you'd be good for my best friend." I overhear him whisper to her and I smile. He did, it's true. Even before the accident, when he found a photo of her on my phone and I finally admitted my feelings for his sister, he punched me then told me not to hurt her.

It took time for me to come to terms with people knowing about my love for the blond beauty. All the time I'd known her she was off-limits, she was too young and I wasn't going to do anything to jeopardize my life and hers, so we remained friends for two long years.

"Let's eat," Piper announces excitedly, her bare feet pattering on the tiled floor as she heads to the kitchen. When she returns carrying two large bowls filled with different salads, we follow her to the table and settle ourselves. "Drinks?"

"I'll have that lemonade you made last night," I respond.

"The same for me." Preston looks over at me with a smirk. "I'm done, man. It's time we all took a healthier route."

"Who are you and what have you done with my best friend?"

He chuckles. "He's your brother now too,

so you'd better get used to that shit."

"I wouldn't have it any other way," I tell him.

With Piper at the school getting ready for the showcase, I've decided to hang back at the apartment to pack my things. I wanted to stay here longer, but there's a building that's just been put up for sale and if I don't head out to put an offer in, I may miss it.

Tomorrow morning, we'll head back to LA for a week before Piper will come home to finish up her studies. Two months and she'll be living with me in the City of Angels. The one place I lost my youth, but it's also the place I plan to build a forever in.

Checking the time, I realize I have to leave soon and head down to the school to watch Piper's class. I'm excited and nervous. I want to be up there, with her, but I know I won't be able to get through it.

Grabbing my keys, I head out the door and I'm on my way moments later. As the school comes into view, I notice all the cars parked along the sidewalk. One that's missing is her father's. I can't believe he's still holding a grudge.

When I step into the hall, I realize how many people are actually here.

"Ryder." I'm surprised to I hear my father's voice call out to me. "Sit with me."

And I do. Settling beside him, I notice he's not in his suit, but a pair of faded blue jeans and a white shirt.

"I didn't know you'd be here," I tell him as they set up the stage.

"Your girl is something else, Ryder." His voice is filled with pride. "She sent me an invite and told me you might need someone to sit with. She also told me about what happened with her folks. They confessed. I know you may be angry with me," he says, turning to me. "But after your mother left, I was lost, stupidly so. And I made a mistake." The regret in his eyes is palpable, and I realize we all make mistakes. I've made my share of them, but forgiveness is better to live with than anger.

"Thanks for being here."

It's all I can offer him for now. But he nods, and we settle in for the show.

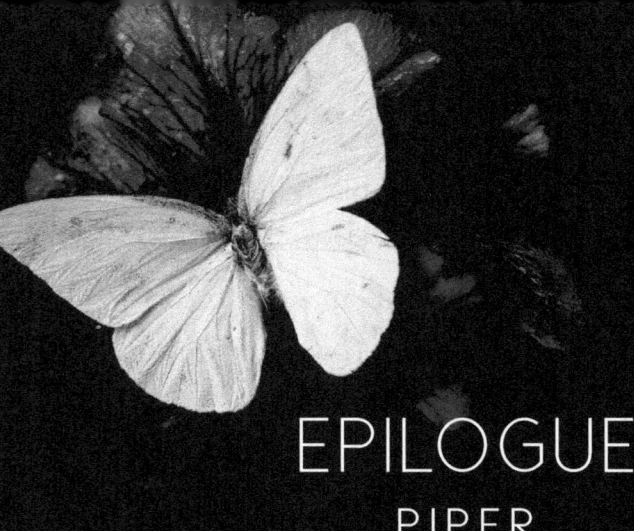

EPILOGUE
PIPER

"Are you going to finish up today?"

He sighs over the line, and I know I've asked him this a hundred times before, but I'm excited to see what he's been working on. Ryder told me I'm not allowed to become his wife until we're both ready, and I am. But we waited until our studio is off the ground and it's become one of the most successful dance studios in Los Angeles.

"Ryder, ignoring me isn't going to make me go away." I know I sound like a nag, but I can't help my excitement.

"Baby girl," he growls down the line, which does funny things to my belly and sends a tingle of electricity between my legs. "I'll be home in an hour, and if you're not naked on our bed, I'll rip those clothes off with my teeth."

"Sex isn't always the answer, Ryder," I retort playfully, earning me another panty-melting growl down the line. I'm about to continue my tirade when suddenly the door flies open and he saunters inside with a bouquet of bright red roses.

"What are you doing here?"

"You're not naked."

"That wasn't an hour," I bite back, knowing it will earn me a night of him keeping me on edge while he licks and kisses every inch of my body.

"Butterfly," he says. The warning tone of his voice tells me I should head to the bedroom, but the roses he hands me steal my attention. There are a dozen beautiful buds and they smell incredible. "I wanted to wish you happy anniversary, so I bought some flowers. I heard women like this shit."

Rolling my eyes, I pin him with a glare. "It's not shit, and yes, women like it, but your fiancée loves it, and she loves you too."

"I know she loves me," he coos. His hands grip my hips and lifts me up. The flowers find a place on the countertop and I'm taken into the bedroom. "And I'm about to show her just how much I love her."

"You can't right now," I inform him with a pout.

"Why the fuck not?"

"Preston and Jeremiah are coming over for dinner with their dates."

At that news, he groans in frustration, and I know why because I can feel his erection at my core, ready to slide into me, but we don't have time.

"You know, baby girl..." Ryder's gaze

locks on mine, and I suck in a breath. There's so much more emotion in the way he looks at me than ever before. He's always stolen my breath, he's always been the beat to my heart, but right here, at this moment, I know he'll be my forever. "You're the woman I was made for."

"And you, Mr. Kingsley," I whimper when he presses his cock against my body. "Are the only man I was born to love."

I cup his face in my hands, pulling him closer until our lips touch. It's a gentle kiss, nothing hungry about it. It's a classical song playing loud and clear, rather than the rhythm filled bass of a hip-hop song. But even though he changes the music on me every day, Ryder is the only man who knows how to make my heart dance wildly and unconstrained.

"I love you more than a love song," he whispers.

"Well, you're soon going to need to love

two of us, rather than just one."

He stills for a moment, not quite getting what I mean. Realization filters over his expression and his eyes fill with glistening tears.

"Do you mean what I think you mean?" His voice is husky when he asks me.

"Yes, we're going to be parents."

At that, he spins me around and I'm dizzy with happiness, and with a heart filled with more love than I ever thought possible.

"I fucking love you, my perfect soon-to-be wife." His husky growl makes me tremble.

"And I fucking love you, my flawed, yet perfect soon-to-be husband," I tell him, kissing him fully on the mouth. His tongue dances with mine just like our bodies do.

Flawed, yet perfect in our imperfections.

ACKNOWLEDGMENTS
THANK YOU

This story was one helluva ride. It started out slow, easy writing, but then Ryder hit me with a plot twist I didn't see coming. And I knew that somehow, I needed to get through it. Both he and Piper left me in tears, but ultimately, happy tears that they could love each other unconditionally.

Thank you Emily for your hard work in polishing these two characters for me!

Thank you to the four ladies who helped BETA this story—Alicia, Allyson, Cat, and Sheena—I can't imagine what I'd do without you!

A huge thanks to my my Angels street team—

Tre, Sheena, Sarah, Lisa, Caroline, TJ, Hayfaah, Joy, Cinders, Fran, Erin, Tanya—thank you for pimping my work EVERYWHERE. You ladies rock!!

Yo my PA who's taken over the reigns to keep me in check, Diane, thank you for everything! You've been a godsend!

My reader group, The Darklings, as always, you're the only place I know I'll find like-minded ladies and a handful of gents who will have a laugh without drama. The group has grown so much and I'm excited for the future! Thank you for being there.

To all my author colleagues, thank you for always sharing, commenting, and supporting me. I appreciate every one of you. Having a support system is important and you ladies provide that and so much more.

Readers and bloggers, from the bottom of my little black heart, THANK YOU. All you do for us authors is incredible. Reading and reviewing is demanding on your own time and you do it with a smile. Thank you so, so much. You are valued and appreciated for taking time out to show us so much love.

If you enjoyed this story, please consider leaving a review. I'd love you forever. (Even though I already do!)

PLAYLIST
THE MUSIC

Dance Like We're Making Love - Ciara

Na Na - Trey Songz

Cookie - R. Kelly

Perfect - Ed Sheeran

Ride it - Jay Sean

Unsteady - X Ambassadors

You're Beautiful - James Blunt

Dancing with Your Ghost - No Resolve

I Got You - Corvyx

Run - Leona Lewis

Because of You - Kelly Clarkson

Losing You - Witt Lowry (feat. Max)

Rockstar - Post Malone (feat. 21 Savage)

Shape of You - Ed Sheeran

Silhouette - Aquilo

One Track Mind - Thirty Seconds to Mars
(feat. A$AP Rocky)

No Te Quiero - Sophia Del Carmen

I Mean It - G-Eazy

Let's Get Lost - G-Eazy

Kiss Me Through The Phone - Soulja Boy,
Sammie

Find me on Spotify for the full list

ABOUT
THE AUTHOR

Dani is a USA Today Bestselling Author of dark and deviant romance with a seductive edge.

Originally from Cape Town, South Africa, she now lives in the UK with her better half who does all the cooking while she writes all the words.

When she's not writing, she can be found binge-watching the latest TV series, or working on graphic design either for herself, or other indie authors.

She enjoys reading books about handsome villains and feisty heroines, mostly dark, always seductive, and sometimes depraved. She has a healthy addiction to tattoos, coffee, and ice cream.

You can find more information on her website, www.danirene.com, or find her on social media, Instagram and Facebook being her favorites. Along with her newsletter, which you can sign up for here - https://bit.ly/DaniVIPs

OTHER BOOKS

BY DANI

or more of my titles, please visit my website
www.danirene.com

FIND ME
ONLINE

Do you follow me?
If not, head over to any of the below links,
I love to hear from my readers!

Amazon
BookBub
Facebook
Facebook Group
Goodreads
Twitter
Pinterest
Instagram
Website & Store
Newsletter
Spotify